# The Case of the

# Overdue
# Otterhound

*A Thousand Islands Doggy Inn Mystery*

# B.R. Snow

ISBN: 978-1-942691-42-6

Website: www.brsnow.net/

Twitter: @BernSnow

Facebook: facebook.com/bernsnow

Cover Design: Reggie Cullen

Cover Photo: James R. Miller

# Other Books by B.R. Snow

### *The Thousand Islands Doggy Inn Mysteries*

- The Case of the Abandoned Aussie
- The Case of the Brokenhearted Bulldog
- The Case of the Caged Cockers
- The Case of the Dapper Dandie Dinmont
- The Case of the Eccentric Elkhound
- The Case of the Faithful Frenchie
- The Case of the Graceful Goldens
- The Case of the Hurricane Hounds
- The Case of the Itinerant Ibizan
- The Case of the Jaded Jack Russell
- The Case of the Klutz King Charles
- The Case of the Lovable Labs
- The Case of the Mellow Maltese
- The Case of the Natty Newfie

### *The Whiskey Run Chronicles*

- Episode 1 – The Dry Season Approaches
- Episode 2 – Friends and Enemies
- Episode 3 – Let the Games Begin
- Episode 4 – Enter the Revenuer
- Episode 5 – A Changing Landscape
- Episode 6 – Entrepreneurial Spirits
- Episode 7 – All Hands On Deck
- The Whiskey Run Chronicles – The Complete Volume 1

### *The Damaged Posse*

- American Midnight
- Larrikin Gene
- Sneaker World
- Summerman
- The Duplicates

### *Other Books*

- Divorce Hotel
- Either Ore

*To Karen and Drew*

# *Chapter 1*

Although I'm sure many of you will disagree, as well as have some serious concerns about my sanity, sitting in a boat fishing for Northern Pike two days before Christmas in a light snow that's defenseless against a stiff breeze out of the north is a perfectly normal and relaxing way to spend the afternoon. Besides, the sun was peeking through the clouds, and I was dressed for the elements and catching more than enough fish to keep me focused and my mind off the cold. I should also mention my good friend Rooster had brought along a thermos of hot coffee laced with brandy that warmed my insides and left me with a contented smile. Of course, like any sane person, I would have preferred to be out here in shorts and a tee shirt in eighty-degree weather with a full picnic basket and a cooler packed with cold beverages, but I was still in a boat on the magnificent St. Lawrence with a fishing pole in my hands, my Christmas shopping finished, and only good thoughts on my mind.

And it sure beats battling hordes of last-minute shoppers at the mall.

By the time Thanksgiving had come and gone, I'd been certain Clay Bay and the surrounding areas were destined for record snowfall and temperatures cold enough to stop time. But about a week ago, it had warmed, and much of the snow had melted. And when Rooster called this morning inviting me to join him for a final day on the River before winter did arrive in full-force, I quickly agreed.

I glanced over the side of the boat and studied the clear bottom. At the moment, the water is shallow here in Weasel Creek, a section of the River separated from deep water by a stretch of marshland that begins at the shoreline and extends out a couple hundred yards before forming an L that runs horizontally offshore for about a mile. As such, it's the perfect sanctuary for pike and other fish looking for warmer water - a relative term at this time of year in our little corner of the world - and a place to lay low for the winter.

Soon, the entire area where Rooster's boat was gently rocking would become a thick sheet of ice, and dozens of ice fishermen would arrive on snowmobiles and ATVs to try their luck catching hungry Northern Pike by drilling holes for their tip-ups. But today, we were the only game in town, and the fish seemed to have figured that out judging by the way they were going after the snacks I was dangling in front of them. I had no idea why the fish were avoiding Rooster's offerings like the plague, and I was doing my best not to laugh every time he muttered under his breath about his lack of success.

I felt a hard tug on my line, and I swiveled my seat ninety-degrees.

"Another one?" Rooster said, glancing over at me with a frown.

"Yeah," I said, starting to reel the fish in. "A big one, I think."

"That's five in the last hour and a half," he said, shaking his head.

"Six," I said, flashing him a grin. "But who's counting?"

I continued to reel the line in. About thirty feet from the boat, the fish broke through the shallow water, and we got a good look at it.

"Wow. Did you see the size of him?"

"I did," he said. "Life is so unfair."

I kept my line tight as I continued to reel the fish toward the boat. Rooster grabbed a net and slowly inched his way next to me to keep the boat steady since nothing ruins an early-winter fishing trip faster than falling overboard into frigid water barely above freezing. I maneuvered the fish next to the boat, and Rooster scooped it into the net then set it down on the deck. We both stared down at the flopping Northern.

"Look at the size of him," Rooster said.

"He's huge," I said, reaching for the fish and the hook that was set hard in its mouth. "Hang on, big guy. I won't be a sec."

"Don't talk to the fish, Suzy," Rooster said. "It's weird."

"Suzy, six. Rooster, nada," I said, grinning at him. "Need I say more?"

"It's still weird," he said, watching me as I tucked the fish under an arm and used the other to gently remove the hook.

"There you go," I said, leaning over the edge of the boat and sliding the fish in the water. I shuddered when my hands dipped below the surface. Moments later, the fish found its bearings, and I let go. It disappeared with a flick of its tail. "Nice fish. He must have been close to fifteen pounds."

"I can't believe you let him go," Rooster said.

"Since I don't eat them, there's no reason to keep them."

"Yeah, but I do," Rooster said, shaking his head. "And he would have looked great in my smoker. Or on my grill."

"You know our deal, Rooster. You can eat all the fish you want, just not the ones I catch."

"You are so weird," he said, shaking his head as he refilled my cup.

We both looked up when we heard a single gunshot that reverberated across the water, and we glanced in the direction the sound had come from.

"Somebody's out hunting," Rooster said.

"That sounded like a rifle," I said. "Deer season's over, right?"

"Yeah, but we're still in the middle of critter season," Rooster said as he jerked his fishing pole then shook his head. "Dang it, I lost another one."

"Critter season?" I said, raising an eyebrow at him.

"Yeah, you know. Weasel, coyote, bobcat, raccoon. Critters."

"Got it."

"Or it could be somebody who doesn't pay attention to the official hunting seasons," he said, still glancing around. "I thought we'd be the only idiots out here today."

"Have you decided if you're going to visit us in Cayman this year?" I said, rebaiting my hook and casting.

"I think I will," he said. "How does sometime in late January sound?"

"Perfect. Come down whenever you want," I said, taking a sip of my *coffee*. "You want to stay at our place?"

"Your Mom has been pretty insistent that I stay with her and Paulie."

"Okay," I said, glancing over at him. "But the food's better at our place."

"I think I can walk the quarter-mile down the beach."

"It'll be great to have you there," I said. "We'll go deep sea fishing. Maybe you'll have better luck." I flashed him an evil grin. "There must be a ton of fish out there for you not to catch."

"When do you guys leave?"

"Two days after Christmas."

"Good," Rooster deadpanned.

I made a face at him and took another sip.

"It's too bad the Chief had to cancel," I said. "He was looking forward to coming out with us."

"Duty calls, right?"

"No, actually my mother called," I said, laughing. "She and the rest of the town council wanted to go through next year's budget again."

"Yuk," Rooster said, frowning.

"Yeah, I know. Come on, Rooster," I said, nodding out at the water. "Hurry up and get a fish. I've got a plane to catch in a couple of days." Then I felt my line jerk again. "Well, what do you know? Another bite."

"I don't believe it."

"Here," I said, offering him my pole. "It's sort of cheating, but my feet are starting to get numb."

"I'm not proud," he said, taking it and beginning to reel the fish in.

My phone buzzed, and I grabbed it from my coat pocket. I checked the number then answered.

"Hey, Chief," I said. "How's the meeting going?"

"Don't ask," he said. "At the moment, we're half an hour into a debate about whether or not to raise the parking meter rates by a quarter."

"Brutal," I said, laughing. "So, what's up?"

"I just got a call from Peggy Jones," the Chief said.

"Sure, I know Peggy," I said, scanning the horizon. "Actually, we're fishing not far from her place."

"Yeah, that's what I thought," Chief Abrams said. "She called to report what she thinks is an animal in distress."

"What sort of animal?" I said, frowning.

"She's not sure," the Chief said. "At first, Peggy thought it was a dog, but then she started hearing what she describes as a loud baying sound that's been going on for about twenty minutes. She says it sounds like a howling cry for help."

"The poor thing," I said. "Did she say if it sounds like the animal is moving, or do the howls seem to be coming from the same spot?"

"She didn't say. Would that make any difference?"

"Not necessarily," I said. "But there are some trappers who work around this area. Maybe the animal got caught in a trap."

"Yeah, that's a possibility," the Chief said. "Anyway, I can't get out of here at the moment, and I was wondering if you and Rooster could check it out."

"Sure," I said, glancing at Rooster who was holding a net with a large Northern in it. "Actually, your timing is perfect. Rooster just caught a fish. Finally."

"Funny," Rooster said, removing the hook and sliding the fish into a large cooler. "What's up?"

"Chief says there's an animal in distress near Peggy Jones' place."

"Okay, let's go check it out," Rooster said, putting his pole away and firing up the engine.

"We're on it, Chief," I said.

"Thanks," Chief Abrams said. "Peggy says it sounds like the animal is somewhere in the marsh that runs offshore in front of her property."

"I'll let you know what we find," I said. "And if my mother is worried about finding more revenue, just tell her to pay her unpaid parking tickets."

"You think I've suddenly developed a death wish?"

"Coward."

"Absolutely."

# Chapter 2

Rooster accelerated, and I hunkered down to protect myself from the chill as best I could. But by the time we left the confines of Weasel Creek and reached deep water, my teeth were chattering, and I was officially freezing my butt off. Rooster headed downriver for about a mile then turned into another area of marshland similar to the one we'd just come from. At the entrance to the bay known as Willow Place, he put the boat in neutral, and we listened closely. We drifted for several minutes surrounded by a silence broken only by the sound of the wind. Then off in the distance to our right, we heard what sounded like muffled whimpers and a howl that reminded me of a Bloodhound's.

"Definitely a dog," I said, nodding at Rooster.

"Yeah, you're right," he said, accelerating slowly.

He steered the boat slowly along the perimeter of the decayed brown marsh. A dusting of snow and ice had collected where the water met land, and we scanned the area for signs of the dog.

"It's hard to see anything," I said, squinting. "Everything blends together. You wouldn't happen to have a pair of binoculars, would you?"

"No, I didn't bring them with me," he said, staring out at the water.

"I can't hear over the sound of the engine," I said. "Let's drift for a few minutes."

Rooster shut the motor off, and the silence returned. We continued to drift, then I heard a whimpered howl that was definitely louder than the previous ones.

"Okay, we're close," Rooster said, grabbing an oar and starting to pole the boat forward in the shallow water.

Moments later, I caught a glimpse of a dog stretched out on the frozen ground, its back paws dangling in the water. It turned its head and noticed us then let loose with an extended wail that broke my heart.

"The poor thing must be freezing to death," I said, scanning the area for a landing spot.

"Why the heck isn't it moving?" Rooster said, pointing the bow toward shore.

"It looks like it might be stuck," I said, then grimaced when I caught a glimpse of steel reflecting in the sun. "Oh, no. Its front left leg is definitely caught in a trap."

"Probably muskrat," Rooster said, poling faster. "This is a popular spot for trappers. But what the heck is a dog doing out here?"

"I have no idea," I said, sitting down to remove my boots.

"What are you doing?" Rooster said.

"I'm going to get the dog," I said, rolling up my pants as far as they would go.

"Suzy, that would be just about the dumbest thing you've ever done."

"Not even close," I said, climbing up and sitting on the edge of the boat with my feet dangling close to the surface of the frigid water.

"Hang on," Rooster said, maneuvering the boat as close as he could to the dog. "Let me give you a hand."

"No, I've got it," I said, then paused. "How do I open the trap?"

"We'll need to open the spring mechanism," he said, removing his work boots. "But those traps are hard to work with, and there's no way you'll be able to handle it and the dog by yourself." He took a deep breath then exhaled loudly. "Okay, let's get this over with."

We both slowly lowered ourselves into the water and gasped when it reached our knees.

"Oh, my word," I said. "I can't believe how cold this water is."

"Yeah, tell me about it," Rooster said, taking a step forward. "When are we going to Cayman?"

"Not soon enough," I said, my neurons on fire from the cold and pain.

We crossed the ten-foot gap between the boat and land with three giant steps and Rooster climbed up onto the bank then extended a hand and pulled me out of the water.

"Be careful," Rooster said as we approached the dog who was staring at us, obviously in pain and shivering uncontrollably from fear and the cold.

"Do you think there are other traps around here?" I said, surveying the ground as I slowly approached the dog.

"There could be," Rooster said. "But I was referring to the dog. It's obviously traumatized."

"I'll be fine," I said, glancing back at him as I reached a hand out to pet the dog's back leg.

Then I felt a pain that momentarily made me forget about the numbness in my legs. I screamed and snatched my hand back, then stared down at the raw flesh and blood pouring from the dog bite I'd just received.

"Ow. Geez, that hurts," I said, squeezing my hand tight. "Now *that* was one of the dumbest things I've ever done."

"Here," Rooster said, holding out a bandana. "Put your hand in there."

I did, and he quickly wrapped the bandana tight around my hand and tied it off. Blood quickly began seeping through it.

"You're gonna need stitches," Rooster said. "And we're both going to be popsicles if we don't get this done soon."

"Let me try this again," I said, kneeling down close to the dog but out of reach of its snapping jowls. "It's okay," I whispered to the dog. "Easy does it. That's it. Good girl. Who's the good girl?"

The dog stopped snarling but remained on edge as my hand again landed on her back leg. But she didn't try to bite me again. I glanced up at Rooster who was hovering right behind me.

"I'll try to hold her while you get the trap open," I said, slowly inching closer to the dog's head. I extended my good hand, hoped like hell I wouldn't lose it in the process, and rested it gently on the dog's head. "Good girl. Who's the good girl?"

The dog sniffed my hand, then managed a soft lick, and I relaxed.

"Hang in there," I whispered as an extended bout of shivers went through me. "We're going to get you out of there." I slowly and gently wrapped both arms around the dog and waited until she relaxed. "Yeah, that feels good, doesn't it?" I nodded at Rooster, and he stepped around the dog and reached for the trap. Moments later, he had it open, and he slowly removed the dog's front left leg then let the trap snap shut.

"How bad does it look?" I said, rubbing the dog's head.

"It's pretty mangled," Rooster said, shaking his head. "But at least it's not one of those traps with teeth. It doesn't look she's bleeding much."

"What kind of trap is it?"

"Definitely muskrat," Rooster said. "Okay, let's get her back to the boat and get out of here. You want me to carry her?"

"No, since she's calmed down, let's not take the chance of riling her up again," I said, looking around as I tried to figure out a game plan for how I was going to pull it off.

"She's a pretty big dog," Rooster said. "Are you sure you're going to be able to lift her?"

"I'm going to have to, right?" I said, carefully placing my arms underneath the dog and flinching as I waited for her response. "Good girl."

"See if you can do it without getting your face bitten off," Rooster said.

"Thanks, Coach," I said, lifting the dog and standing up on the frozen ground. "Turn the stern around. I'll see if I can set her down on the back cushion."

"Hang on," Rooster said, stepping back into the water and gasping. He grabbed the side of the boat and turned it until the stern was facing me, about five feet away. "Watch that first step. It really gets your attention."

"Yeah, thanks for the warning," I said, stepping into the water clutching the dog with both arms. "Oh, that's brutal." I took a small step, then another, and lifted the dog onto the boat and set her down on the padded cushion that ran across the stern. "Good girl."

Rooster climbed into the boat, extended a hand and pulled me in. I landed with a thud on the deck, soaked from the waist down and colder than I'd ever been in my life. He grabbed a stack of towels and blankets, and I wrapped one of the blankets around me then headed for the dog. I gently dried the shivering dog with a towel, then used a second to finish the job. I wrapped a blanket around the dog leaving only her head exposed. The dog whimpered and continued to shake from the cold, but the howling had stopped.

"Okay," Rooster said. "Take your pants off."

"Oh, Rooster. You're such a sweet talker," I deadpanned as I caught the pair of sweatpants he tossed to me. "How come you have extra clothes on the boat?"

"For times like this, why do you think?" he said, also changing into a pair of sweats. Then he threw a pair of wool socks to me. "Get those on and try to keep them as dry as possible."

I pulled the thick socks on and immediately felt a bit better as my feet began to warm up.

"How she's doing?" Rooster said, firing up the engine.

"It's too early to tell," I said, cradling the dog in my arms as I shivered uncontrollably. "Let's get going, okay?"

"Yeah," Rooster said, accelerating before coming to an abrupt stop and backing the boat up. "Hang on."

"Rooster, we're both about fifteen minutes from the onset of severe hypothermia," I snapped. "Let's go."

"Wait," he said, scanning the withered marsh then pointing. "Look over there. About forty-five degrees, starboard."

I followed his arm, scanned the area, then grimaced. I hugged the dog tighter and did my best to ignore the throbbing pain in my legs.

"Is that a hand sticking up out of the water?" I whispered.

"It certainly is," Rooster said, again removing his boots. "Now we know why the dog was out here. Probably her owner. I'll be right back."

"Be careful," I said, reaching for my phone.

Rooster removed his sweatpants and socks, slid back into the water and waded his way onto solid ground. I watched as he grabbed the man's hand and pulled the body out of the water onto a section of trampled, semi-frozen marshland. He flipped the body over and shook his head. Despite his reputation as a man who could deal with whatever Mother Nature decided to throw his way, Rooster was shaking from head to toe.

"He's dead, right?" I said, hugging the dog tighter as much for my own warmth as hers.

"Yeah, he certainly is," Rooster said, glancing around, apparently unsure about his next move. "He's still bleeding from the shoulder, but I'm gonna guess the shot knocked him into the water and he drowned."

"I'll call the Chief," I said. "But we can't sit here and wait for him. We have to get the dog to Josie, and we need to dry off before we freeze to death."

"Yeah, I know," Rooster said. "Toss me one of those wet towels."

I let go of the dog and shivered uncontrollably as I grabbed a towel from the deck, got to my feet and tossed it toward him. It landed with a splash near the bank, and Rooster grabbed it then tied it to a dead branch about three feet off the ground.

"Can you see that?" he said.

"I can," I said, dialing the Chief's number. "Let's go. Get back in the boat. There's nothing more you can do for him at the moment."

I sat back down and hugged the dog with both arms. She was still shaking and whimpering. Rooster made the short trip back through the shallow water and climbed into the boat. He dried himself off the best he could, then put the sweats and socks back on. The Chief finally answered on the fifth ring.

"Hey," Chief Abrams said. "What's up?"

"We've got a problem here," I said. "Actually, several."

"What happened?" he said, concerned.

Rooster fired up the engine and pressed the throttle hard. The boat accelerated and planed over. He glanced over his shoulder and yelled to make himself heard over the roar.

"Your place, right?"

I nodded as another wave of shivers came over me. Then I remembered the dog bite. I glanced down at the bandana wrapped around my hand and realized it was dripping blood.

"Suzy? Are you still there?" the Chief said.

"Yeah. Look, you need to grab Freddie and get out to Willow Place right away," I yelled above the roar of the engine, hugging the dog tight.

"I need to grab Freddie?" he said, his voice deflated.

"I'm afraid so," I said. "We won't be here, but you'll see a light green towel tied to a branch about a quarter-mile down from the deep-water entrance on the right."

"Who is it?" Chief Abrams said.

"Actually, that's a good question," I said, frowning. "I have no idea." I lowered the phone and yelled to Rooster. "Do you know who the victim is?"

"I do," Rooster called back without slowing down. "It's Skitch Friendly."

The last name registered briefly, but no one specific came to mind.

"It's somebody named Skitch Friendly," I said to the Chief.

"Skitch Friendly?" the Chief said. "I thought he was dead."

"He is. I just told you that," I said, rubbing the dog's head with my bandaged hand and getting blood all over her.

"Don't start," the Chief said. "What else is going on? You said you had more than one problem."

"The noise that Peggy reported was actually a dog that got her leg caught in a muskrat trap," I said. "We're on our way to the Inn so Josie can take a look at her."

"Poor thing," the Chief said. "Anything else?"

"Rooster and I got soaked trying to rescue her."

18

"You guys went in the water?" the Chief said.

"We did."

"Are you out of your mind?"

"Yeah, I'm almost positive," I said, shivering and leaning down to block the wind the best I could. "Oh, and the dog bit me."

"*You* got bit by a dog? Where?"

"On the hand," I said.

"Unbelievable," he said. "How's the dog doing?"

"Better than I am at the moment," I said, trying to stop my teeth from chattering. "But she's in pretty bad shape."

"Don't worry, Josie will work her magic," the Chief said. "Okay, be safe and try to stay warm. I'll track Freddie down."

"Sorry to drag you out here," I said.

"Well, at least it gets me out of the meeting," the Chief said, managing a small laugh. "Do you want me to say anything to your mother?"

"No, you better let me handle it," I said.

"Okay. I'll touch base with you later, and we'll compare notes," the Chief said.

"Got it. Thanks, Chief."

"How cold is the water?"

"You wouldn't believe me if I told you."

# Chapter 3

Rooster pulled into our dock in front of the Inn where Sammy and Jill were waiting with a stack of blankets and towels. Jill grabbed the bow and Sammy headed for the stern where I was standing with the dog in my arms. She was still shivering and growled when Sammy reached out with both hands. Then he caught a glimpse of my bandaged hand and pulled his arms back.

"Did she do that to you?" Sammy said, nodding at the blood-soaked bandana.

"Yeah, be careful," I said, extending the dog toward him. "Good girl. Who's the good girl?"

"She's shaking like a leaf," Sammy said, again reaching out. "And you're doing a pretty good job yourself. What happened?"

"Sammy, I'm really not in the mood to chat," I snapped, my arms cramping from the dog's weight.

Sammy knelt down, accepted the dog from me, and grimaced as he waited for the dog's reaction. But the dog had apparently decided we were there to help her, and she relaxed into Sammy's arms. He immediately started down the dock and then up the small incline that led to the Inn.

"Is Josie ready for her?" I said to Jill.

"She is," Jill said, then glanced at Rooster. "You want me to tie the boat off?"

"No, thanks," Rooster said. "I need to get home to shower and warm up. But you need to give Suzy a hand getting out of the boat."

Jill did, and I stood shivering on the dock as Rooster backed the boat out.

"I'll give you a call later," Rooster said. "If I make it."

"Don't even joke about that," I said, frowning at him. "Hey, we're having dinner with my mom at C's tonight. Why don't you join us?"

"What time?"

"Seven."

"Good Lord willing, I'll be there," he called out as he accelerated and headed off with a wave.

"Let's get you inside," Jill said, draping a blanket over my shoulders as we headed down the dock.

I moved as fast as my cold, cramping legs would allow, and I eventually made it up the front steps and waited for Jill to open the door. I stepped inside and was greeted by all four house dogs. Chloe, my Aussie Shepherd, immediately sensed something was wrong and maintained contact with my legs until I sat down. She hopped up on the chair next to mine and draped her head in my lap. Jill knelt down in front of me, removed my socks, then reached under my spacious sweatpants and began vigorously massaging my feet and calves. Michele, one of our staff members, entered the registration area carrying a steaming mug of tea, and I slowly sipped it as Jill continued to squeeze and rub my feet and lower legs.

"Ow," I said, wincing.

"You feel that?" Jill said, glancing up.

"Well, yeah," I snapped.

"Good. That's what we want," she said, continuing her forceful massage. "We need to get the blood flowing."

A few minutes later, she stopped and stood.

"Try walking around a bit," Jill said.

I took a few tentative steps, then gently bounced up and down on my feet.

"Well done," I said, nodding. "But has anybody ever mentioned that you have the hands of a steelworker?"

"Okay, she's back," Jill said, grinning at Michele. "You should head up to the house and take a long, hot shower."

"No, I need to see how the dog is doing. Where's Josie?"

"Exam room 3," Jill said. "Let me at least bring you some dry clothes."

"That you can do," I said, taking a moment to pet all four dogs before gingerly heading toward the exam room.

Inside, Josie and Inga, one of our newer techs, had the dog stretched out on a table. She was wrapped in warm blankets, and Inga had her hands underneath them and was massaging the dog's back legs.

"Hey," Josie said, glancing up when I entered. "How was your swim?"

"Just peachy," I said, making a face at her. "How's she doing?"

"She's one lucky dog," Josie said. "If you guys hadn't found her, she'd be a popsicle by now. Good job."

"Thanks," I said, gently rubbing the dog's head.

Jill entered carrying a bowl, and I recognized the smell immediately.

"That's Chef Claire's chicken and carrot broth, isn't it?" I said, my stomach rumbling.

"It is," Jill said. "I stuck it in the microwave. I think it's warm enough."

Josie stuck the tip of her finger into the bowl and nodded.

"That's fine," Josie said. "Let's see if she'll drink it."

Jill set the bowl down on the exam table, and the dog lifted its head then began lapping up the warm broth.

"She likes it," Jill said.

"Good," Josie said. "That should help get her core temp back up."

"Did you get an x-ray yet?"

"I did," Josie said, pulling back one of the blankets to check the dog's abdomen. "Her leg is broken right above the paw. Her carpals are pretty much snapped in half."

"But you can fix it with surgery, right?" I said, noticing the hot water bottle resting on the dog's stomach.

"I can," Josie said, nodding. "I'll probably need to put a plate in there, so there goes her dance career. But it's better than losing the leg."

"When will she be ready for surgery?" I said.

"It's hard to say," Josie said, glancing at me. "But I'm gonna say a week, maybe two."

"What?" I said, frowning at her.

Josie reached down and removed the hot water bottle. I stared at the dog's distended abdomen.

"She's pregnant?" I said, stunned.

"Very much so," Josie said, sliding the water bottle back in place.

"How the heck did I miss that?"

"I imagine you were a little preoccupied trying to save her life," Josie said, shrugging. "But there's no way I'm going to put her under until she delivers her litter. The anesthesia could kill the pups." Josie placed her stethoscope on the dog's chest and listened carefully for several seconds. "Her vitals are pretty good considering what she went through. After her core temp is back to normal, I'll get a splint on the leg to immobilize it, then we'll get her into a condo and give her a mild sedative."

"The poor thing," I said, shaking my head.

"What kind of dog is she?" Inga said.

"Otterhound," Josie and I said in unison.

"I don't think I've ever seen one before," Inga said, adjusting the blankets.

"You're not alone," Josie said. "There's less than a thousand of them worldwide."

"Yeah, they're pretty rare," I said. "And I had no idea somebody around here had one." I glanced at Josie. "Did you?"

"No," she said, shaking her head. "Jill, she's finished the broth, but it looks like she's still hungry. Why don't you give her a little more?"

"I'll be right back," Jill said, grabbing the empty bowl and heading out the door that led to the back area of the Inn.

"Were they bred to hunt otters?" Inga said. "Is that how they got their name?"

"It is," Josie said, nodding as she stroked the dog's wet beard that hung down from her mouth. "And Otterhounds have a double coat and webbed feet, so they're really good in the water. That double coat might have been what saved her life." She glanced at me. "Apart from you and Rooster, of course."

"We were lucky we were close by," I said, shrugging. "They hunt on scent. I imagine she picked up all sorts of smells in that marsh. She must have been going crazy looking for critters out there."

"I'm sure she was," Josie said. "Speaking of which, did you see the owner?"

"Yeah, I'm pretty sure we saw him," I said, my neurons flaring as I flashed back to the body we'd found.

"What did he have to say?" Josie said, swapping out one of the blankets with a fresh one.

"Not much," I said, using my good hand to help her get the blanket tucked under the dog.

"Well, we'll need to have a chat with him," Josie said. "We've got a lot to talk about."

"That's probably not gonna happen," I said.

"Why not?"

"Because the Chief and Freddie are out there at the moment dealing with him," I said, frowning.

"Really? Another one?" Josie said, scowling.

"I'm afraid so," I said.

"Geez," Josie said, shaking her head. "Should I even ask what happened to him?"

"I really don't know," I said. "But I'm sure we'll be talking about it at dinner."

"Okay," she said, reaching for my bandaged hand. "Let's take a look at that bite."

She gently unwrapped the bandana then tossed it into the trashcan. She lowered an overhead light and switched it on then bent down to take a closer look at my wound.

"Wow, she got you good," Josie said. "You sure you don't want to go to the emergency room?"

"No, that's not necessary," I said. "Just clean and stitch it. And I'm current on my tetanus shot."

"I didn't know vets could work on people," Inga said, frowning.

"It's okay," Josie said, laughing as she rinsed a clean towel in hot water. "Suzy's part dog."

"Funny," I said, making a face at her.

Inga glanced back and forth at us with a confused look on her face.

"How many stitches am I going to need?" I said.

"A lot," she said, grasping my wrist and rolling my hand back and forth. "That's gotta hurt."

"Nothing gets past you."

"Okay, Inga," Josie said, glancing around. "If you and Jill can stay here with her, I'll go sew up the Snoopmeister. Keep swapping out the blankets and the hot water bottle every ten minutes. When I'm done, I'll swing back, and we'll get a splint on that leg. But if her temperature drops or if she starts whimpering or howling, let me know right away."

"Will do," Inga said, moving closer to the dog. "So, she's going to be okay?"

"She's going to be fine," Josie said.

"And her puppies?"

"We're going to have to wait and see about them," Josie said. "But their little heartbeats are all good, so we'll keep our fingers crossed." Josie glanced at me and grinned. "You might be limited to five fingers for a few days."

# Chapter 4

At seven o'clock sharp, we entered C's and headed for the
lounge to say hello to Millie, our head bartender. We sat down at
the bar, and Millie frowned when she saw the bandage on my
hand.

"What on earth happened to you?" she said, pouring two
glasses of Pinot.

"Dog bite," I said, clinking glasses with Josie before taking
a sip.

"*You* got bit by a dog?" she said, surprised. "I guess the end
of the world is coming soon. How many stitches did you get?"

"Nineteen," I said, examining my bandage.

"I was shooting for twenty," Josie deadpanned. "But I just
couldn't make it happen."

I gently punched her shoulder with my good hand, then we
all glanced at the front door when we heard it open. Chief
Abrams and Freddie, our local medical examiner, entered and
removed their coats and gloves. They waved when they saw us
and headed into the lounge.

"Hi, guys," Millie said. "What can I get you?"

"Something that will warm us up," Chief Abrams said. "Do
you have that hot cider tonight?"

"We do," Millie said. "Two?"

"Yes, please," Freddie said, sitting down next to me at the bar. "I heard you got bit by a dog."

I held up my bandaged hand and nodded.

"Wow, wonders never cease," Freddie said, shaking his head. "What did you do? Try to eat out of his bowl?"

Josie and Chief Abrams laughed. I took a sip of wine and ignored him.

"What's the news on the dead guy, Chief?" I said, swiveling my stool toward him.

"Let's wait until we sit down for dinner," the Chief said. "Your mom and Rooster are on their way in, and I really don't feel like telling the story twice."

"Fair enough," I said, nodding. "Did you guys get wet out there?"

"No, we had our rain gear on," the Chief said. "But it sure didn't stop the cold. That water is freezing."

"Brutal," Freddie said. "You and Rooster actually went in? On purpose?"

"Yeah. And Rooster went in twice," I said.

"Yuk," Freddie said with a grimace. "Fortunately, my swimming the next several days will be confined to Miami Beach. I'm headed to a conference."

"What do you do at a medical examiner conference?" I said.

"Talk about dead people," he said with a shrug.

The front door opened again, and my mother and Rooster came in. He helped her with her coat, then removed his. I couldn't help but notice that, instead of his usual habit of underdressing for the weather, Rooster was wearing several layers of clothes.

"Hello, darling," my mother said, giving me a hug and a kiss on the cheek. "Hi, Millie. Josie, gentlemen, it's nice to see you." She reached out and gently grabbed my bandaged hand and examined it. "Are you okay?"

"Yeah, I'm fine," I said. "Josie did a nice job with it."

"You do know that vets aren't supposed to work on people," the Chief said, glancing at Josie.

"Are you going to arrest me, Chief?" she said, laughing.

"Probably not," the Chief said, glancing at my mother. "Given my recent budget cuts, I couldn't afford to feed you."

"Funny," Josie and my mother said in unison.

"Oh, a two for one," I said, laughing. "Well played, Chief."

"How's the dog doing?" Rooster said.

"She's going to be fine," Josie said. "I'm not as sure about how her pups are going to be."

"She's pregnant?" Rooster said. "I didn't even notice."

"Me either," I said, taking a sip of wine.

"Of course, I was a little focused on survival at the time," Rooster said. "I don't think I've ever been that cold before."

"And this coming from a man who doesn't even wear socks in the winter," Josie said.

"Don't worry, I'm wearing them tonight," Rooster said, laughing. "Millie, can I please get a snifter of B&B?"

"Microwaved for twenty seconds, right?" Millie said, reaching for the bottle.

"You're a quick study," Rooster said, glancing at a menu. "Do you know what the soups are tonight?"

"Mulligatawny and New England clam chowder," Josie said.

"Perfect," Rooster said. "It's definitely a soup night."

"Shall we go sit down?" my mother said. "I'm starving."

We grabbed our drinks and followed her into the dining room then sat down at her table near the fireplace. Chief Abrams and Freddie selected the seats closest to the fire and stood close to it to warm up before sitting down. Our server approached and took our orders then headed for the kitchen. Moments later, Chef Claire poked her head out and waved to us then went back to work.

"Okay," Chief Abrams said, placing his elbows on the table. "I assume you'd all like an update."

We sat back in our seats and nodded, nursing our drinks as he spoke.

"As Rooster said, the guy in the marsh was Skitch Friendly," the Chief said.

"Really?" my mother said, surprised. "I didn't think Skitch was still around."

"He liked to spend time on the River," Rooster said. "But you rarely saw him around town."

"What was the cause of death?" I said.

"Well, he had a gunshot wound to the shoulder," Freddie said. "And I'm pretty sure the shot knocked him into the water. Then he drowned."

"What a horrible way to go," Josie said, shaking her head. "Poor guy."

"Yeah," Freddie said. "For his sake, I hope he went quick."

"I wonder if the dog was trying to save him," Rooster said.

"It's possible. Or maybe he was trying to rescue the dog. Where have I heard the name Friendly before?" I said, again trying to retrieve the memory.

"You went to school with his kids for a while," my mother said.

"I did?"

"Yes, a boy and a girl," my mother said. "They were a few years behind you, and I think they left school around junior high."

"I don't remember them," I said, shaking my head.

"Of course, you do, darling. The boy had an oddly-shaped head."

"Oddly-shaped how?"

"It was like it had been *smushed*," my mother said, pressing the tips of her fingers together.

Rooster chuckled and shook his head.

"Smushed. That's a good word for it," he said, taking a sip of his drink.

"It looked like something an abstract painter might come up with," my mother said. "Surely you remember that."

"Of course," I said, nodding. "Cube Head." Then my face flushed red with embarrassment. "That's what the kids called him." I exhaled as a distant memory flashed in my head. "We were pretty mean to him."

"Not your finest moment?" Josie said, glancing over at me.

"Definitely not," I said, frowning. "I can't remember his name."

"Cooter," Rooster said, taking another sip.

"That's cruel," Josie said, shaking her head. "I can't believe his parents called him that."

"Need I remind you that you're talking to a guy named Rooster?" Rooster said.

"He does have a point," I said to Josie.

"I think it's a family name," Rooster said. "But it's probably not the best one they could have stuck him with."

"It's better than Cube Head," Freddie said, shrugging.

"And I remember his sister," I said. "She was a nice girl and really smart. But she also had a strange name."

"Very," Rooster said.

"Yeah, it was very strange," I said, nodding.

"No, that's her name," he said, draining the last of his drink.

"Very Friendly?" Josie said, staring at Rooster. "That was actually her name?"

"That's right," I said. "Very Friendly. I'd completely forgot about those two. Didn't they move out of the area?"

"Not really," Rooster said. "When Skitch's folks died, they left him the family property, and he decided to move the family out there to get away from the rat race."

"Rat race? I must be missing something," Freddie said, frowning. "Clay Bay has a population around 1,500. Where's this rat race he was talking about?"

"He said it got too crowded in the summer," Rooster said. "And Skitch was pretty different from most folks. He was living off the grid before the term got coined. We always used to just call him a hermit."

"And he pulled his kids out of school?" I said.

"Pretty much," Rooster said. "I'd see them occasionally when I went out to his place to do some work on his truck. They've got at least a couple hundred acres in the woods about a half-hour east of town. You need a bloodhound and a group of trackers to find his cabin."

"So, he was like a mountain man?" Josie said.

"If we had any mountains around here, I guess you could call him that," Rooster deadpanned.

"Thanks for the clarification," Josie said, rolling her eyes at him.

"But Skitch was definitely into self-sufficiency. He fished and hunted for food year-round. And he did a lot of trapping and sold the pelts. And knowing Skitch, he probably ate what he caught as well."

"He ate muskrat?" I said, frowning.

"I'm sure he did," Rooster said, shrugging.

"Yuk. Did he have electricity at his place?" I said.

"No, he had a generator he would occasionally use when he absolutely had to. But he had a root cellar he used to store food. Grew his own vegetables in the summer, and canned in the fall. And the cabin has a couple of fireplaces and some wood stoves for cooking and to heat the place."

"Wow," I said as I tried to wrap my head around the lifestyle. "What about running water?"

"Yeah, kinda," Rooster said. "There's a stream running through the place, and a couple of rainwater tanks. It sure isn't how I'd like to live, but if you were going to go off the grid, Skitch had it pretty well worked out."

"So, his family doesn't know he's dead?" my mother said.

"I don't see how they could," Rooster said. "But I'm happy to along with you when you break the news, Chief. The family isn't exactly what I would call cop-friendly."

"I think I'll take you up on that offer, Rooster," the Chief said, taking a sip of his hot cider.

"Me too," I said.

"What?" my mother said, her voice rising a notch. "Just stay out of it, darling. Please."

"No, it's okay, Mom. We need to speak with them about their dog," I said, then frowned. "Assuming that actually is their dog."

"Who else would the dog belong to?" Freddie said.

"I don't know," I said, glancing at Josie. "It just seems really strange that family would own one of the rarest dogs around."

"It certainly does," Josie said. "But you'll have to go by yourself. I need to stick around and keep an eye on the Otterhound."

"They have an Otterhound?" my mother said, raising an eyebrow.

"Yeah," I said.

"That is odd," she said. "I've only seen one once before. A friend of mine in England has one. And it's a lovely dog. What's the one you're taking care of like?"

"She's great," I said. "Smart and a ton of personality. And I'm sure the only reason she bit me was because she was scared to death."

"So, she's friendly?" my mother said.

"Very," Josie deadpanned.

"Don't start," I said, glancing over at her.

"Yeah, like I was going to let that one go."

# Chapter 5

After dinner, we adjourned to the lounge, and I sat down between my mother and Rooster on a couch directly in front of the fire. My hand was starting to throb, and I gently rubbed the bandage.

"Nineteen stitches, huh?" Rooster said.

"Yeah, she got me good," I said, my neurons beginning to flare. "What on earth was he doing with an Otterhound?"

"Obviously hunting critters," Rooster said, shrugging.

"But where did he come across a dog that rare?" I said, still baffled. "You said the guy was basically a hermit."

"Yeah, he was," Rooster said. "But Skitch loved to barter. Maybe somebody paid him for something with the dog."

"Do you think he would have known how rare and valuable that dog is?"

"I'd be surprised if he didn't," Rooster said. "Skitch was pretty sharp."

"Sharp but anti-social," my mother said, glancing at the front door and frowning. "Wonderful. We really need to come up with some rules about who can eat here."

"Who's that?" I said, following my mother's stare.

"Oh, crap, not him," Rooster said, shaking his head.

The man removed his coat, hung it on the rack then entered the lounge and glanced around. Young and smug were the first two words that came to mind. When the man spotted my mother, he headed straight for her.

"Good evening," he said, bowing slightly. "I was hoping to find you here." He glanced around and gave Rooster a small, friendly wave. "Hello, Mr. Jennings." Then his eyes landed on me. He glanced back and forth at me and my mom then spoke to her. "I can't help but notice the resemblance. Let me guess, she's your sister, right?"

"Stuff a sock in it, Mr. Billows," my mother said, then took a sip of coffee.

"Of course," he said. Then he extended his hand toward me. "Herman Billows."

I extended my undamaged left hand, and he grabbed it awkwardly and shook it.

"Suzy."

"It's so nice to meet you, Suzy," Herman Billows said. "That looks like a nasty injury. Did you cut yourself?"

"Bar fight," I deadpanned.

"You should see the other guy," Rooster said with a small grin.

Herman Billows, apparently unsure about whether or not to believe us, smiled nervously as he glanced around the lounge. "I believe I'll have a cocktail. Can I get anyone another drink?"

We shook our heads, and he beamed at us.

"Then please excuse me for a moment while I get one for myself. Don't go anywhere. I'll be right back."

"Wow," I said, shaking my head. "Have you ever met anybody and developed an intense dislike for them immediately?"

"You're an excellent judge of character, darling," my mother said, taking another sip.

"Who on earth is that guy?" I said, glancing over at the bar.

"He is a representative of Eclectic and Easy Energy," my mother said. "Or as our friend Mr. Billows likes to call it, 3E."

"They're big in the fracking market, right?" I said.

"That's the one," Rooster said.

I was somewhat familiar with the drilling technique known as fracking, a controversial process used to harvest natural gas. Basically, you drill straight down into the ground, then horizontally far below the surface. Then a high-pressure mixture of water, sand, and various chemicals with very long names is injected into the rock at high pressure. The pressure creates fractures which release the natural gas. And when the wells are capped and fitted for production, the gas is extracted from the ground similar to how oil is brought to the surface.

Since our area was outside the multitude of fracking zones around the country, we'd been on the periphery of the intense battles the drilling technique had created. Proponents were quick to point out the benefits of natural gas and energy independence. Critics highlighted the environmental problems that could be caused by pumping millions of gallons of water spiked with a wide variety of chemicals, some proven to be carcinogenic, into the ground and potentially into groundwater systems.

I like to consider myself a moderate when it comes to the ongoing debate about the need for growth and development versus protecting the environment. But after I watched a documentary about the dangers of fracking and saw a family that had leased their land hold a cigarette lighter next to a faucet and stared in disbelief as the tap water burst into flames, I definitely moved into the environmental protection camp on this one. In short, the fracking process made me very nervous. But I do understand landowners who decide to lease their land due to the amount of money they can make from lease rights and potential royalties on the extracted gas.

"How do you know this guy, Mom?"

"He came to see me the other day," she said.

"Me too," Rooster said. "The little weasel."

"What on earth would he want to talk with you guys about?" I said, glancing at the bar where Herman Willows was trying, and failing miserably, to chat up Millie.

"He wanted to acquire fracking rights to some of our property," my mother said.

"But that makes no sense," I said, frowning.

"Yes, that's what we thought," my mother said, glancing at Rooster who nodded back at her.

"I've never heard of any natural gas deposits around here," I said. "And New York banned fracking a couple of years ago."

"Bingo," my mother said, beaming at me. "And now you understand our initial confusion, darling."

"Why do I get the feeling there's more to the story?"

"Well, after Rooster and I sent Mr. Billows on his merry way, I decided to call one of my friends in Albany."

"A friend in Albany?" I said, shaking my head. "Let me guess. The Governor?"

"I'd rather not comment on that," she said, turning coy. "Let's just say he's well-placed in the state government and leave it at that."

"So, what did this high-placed official have to say?"

"Apparently, there's been a recent geological find of a natural gas vein that comes out of the Marcellus Shale Formation downstate and runs north."

"As far north as your property?" I said, glancing back and forth at them.

"Some of it, yes," Rooster said.

"But not any of the Riverfront property, right?" I said, my neurons flaring.

"Just a little of it," my mother said, staring at me.

"I'm going to need a little clarification, Mom."

"Apparently, the natural gas vein does extend to the acreage I own that runs along the back of the Inn," she said.

"What?" I said, stunned. "Are you telling me that we could be living next door to a bunch of natural gas wells at some point in the future?"

"No, there's no way I'd let that happen," my mother said. "But Mr. Billows is trying to buy up lease rights on as much land as he can."

"But why?" I said, confused. "The state has banned fracking."

"According to my friend in Albany, several companies, notably 3E, are betting that the state won't be able to sustain its ban for economic and political reasons and will eventually cave. And those companies that have already secured drilling leases will have a major leg up on its competition if that happens."

"That sucks," I said, glaring at Billows' back. "Where's the rest of the property he wants to get his hands on?"

"It's all inland and east from the River," Rooster said. "Mostly wooded areas. But any runoff could potentially damage the groundwater table and maybe end up in the River at some point."

"How much land are we talking about?" I said.

They looked at each other then shrugged.

"It's probably around a couple thousand acres," my mother said, then glanced at Rooster. "That sounds about right, doesn't it?"

"Yeah, probably," he said, nodding. "I really haven't kept close track of it over the years."

"I haven't either," my mother said, then looked at me. "It was pretty much your father's deal."

"Dad bought land in the woods?" I said, frowning.

"Yeah, tons of it," Rooster said. "And he asked me to go in with him and your mom on a few deals. It was a good way to hide some money."

"Hide money?" I said, raising an eyebrow.

"Long story," my mother said, glaring at Rooster.

"Yeah, long story," Rooster said, deflecting. "Anyway, you don't have to worry about it. At least, on our land. We'd never agree to lease it. And since it's going to be yours someday, we know you wouldn't either."

"Why would Dad buy all that land?" I said.

"He liked to walk in the woods," my mother said, shrugging.

"But there could be some people who would agree to lease their property," I said.

"Of course," my mother said. "If they're offered enough money, I'm sure they will."

"But the chances are low that the state will change its mind and make it legal again, right?"

"We're talking about politicians, darling. Certainly, you know by now that anything is possible when it comes to that lot."

We glanced up when Herman Billows approached.

"What did I miss?" he said.

"We were just singing your praises, Mr. Billows," my mother said, smiling up at him.

"I'm sorry I missed it," Billows said. "Does that mean you've changed your mind about my offer?"

"Not a chance," my mother said, maintaining her smile.

"Well, if you do come to your senses, you know where to find me. I'm sure 3E can make it worth your while," he said, draining his drink and giving us a small salute. "Enjoy the rest of your evening."

We watched him depart then settled back on the couch and sipped our drinks.

"And where exactly would you find him, Mom?"

"Well, let's see," she said, reaching into her purse and reading from the business card. "Houston."

"Or the bottom of the River," Rooster said, laughing.

"Now there's an idea," my mother said as she crumpled up the card and tossed it into the fireplace. "Don't give him another thought, darling. I'm sure the cold weather will be enough to drive him away in the very near future."

I spotted Chief Abrams poking his head into the lounge from the dining room and waved. He wandered across the room and stood with his back close to the fire.

"I thought we'd head out to the Friendly's place in the morning," the Chief said. "They're predicting snow in the afternoon."

"That's fine," Rooster said. "What time?"

"Is eight too early?"

"No, that works," Rooster said, glancing over at me. "How about you? Too early?"

"Not at all," I said. "Say, why don't you swing by around seven? I'll make breakfast."

"What are we having?" Josie said, seemingly appearing out of nowhere.

"Somebody's radar is working tonight," I said, laughing.

"Funny," she said, making a face at me. "And I believe you're actually referring to sonar."

"Please promise me you'll be on your best behavior," my mother said.

"Relax, Mom," I said, shaking my head at her. "I'm just tagging along to give them an update on their dog and find out how they'd like to handle a few things."

"Just let the Chief do his thing, and try to remember that the mother has just lost her husband and the kids' father."

"Geez, Mom. I'm not an insensitive idiot."

"I know that, darling. But even you must admit that sometimes you do tend to get carried away."

"Sure, sure."

# Chapter 6

I scarfed down my breakfast then left Rooster and Chief Abrams chatting in the kitchen with Chef Claire while I headed down to the Inn to check in with Josie on the status of the Otterhound. I found her in back inside the dog's condo with the Otterhound stretched out across her lap. Josie had a coffee mug in one hand and was using her free one to gently rub the dog's belly.

"How's she doing?" I said, sitting down on the floor next to her.

"She's a tough girl," Josie said, scratching one of the Otterhound's ears. "Her leg is definitely still hurting, and I wish I could give her something stronger for the pain. But I'm worried about what it might do to the pups."

"You're still getting heartbeats, right?" I said, gently running a hand over the dog's extended stomach.

"I could only hear five this morning," she said, frowning.

"She lost one?" I said, my voice catching in my throat.

"Try not to read too much into it," Josie said. "The pup could have shifted around. Or maybe it's just beating in sync with one of the others."

"But one of them might have died?" I said, tearing up.

"Suzy, it's a miracle the dog survived that ordeal," Josie said, firmly. "But you and Rooster saved her, and now she's resting comfortably with a litter that's getting ready to make their way out into the world. And we'll deal with whatever happens when she delivers. Okay?"

"Yeah," I said, exhaling. "Sorry."

"That's better," she said, sliding out from underneath the dog and gently setting her head down. "While you're out there today, see if you can get her name."

"That I can do."

"Thanks. Now, if you'll excuse me, I have to get ready for Claudius."

I laughed as I stood up. Claudius was a Doberman owned by one of our friends who was due for his annual checkup. And if there was one thing Claudius hated more than getting his shots, it was going to the vet to get them. I followed Josie into the registration area where the very grumpy Doberman had all four legs splayed across the tile floor as his owner tugged the leash and tried to coax the dog to its feet. When he saw Josie in her scrubs, the dog scrambled to his feet and made a dash for the front door.

"It's nice to see you too, Claudius," Josie said, laughing.

"The dog is obviously a good judge of character," I said. "How are you doing, Tess?"

"I'm good," Tess said, struggling to hold onto the leash. "At least I was."

"You all set for Christmas?" I said.

"I think so," Tess said. "Come on, Claudius. Give it a rest," the owner said, shaking her head. "You mind giving me a hand with him, Josie?"

I headed outside to the sound of toenails clicking on tile and low guttural growls. Rooster and the Chief were already waiting for me in the driveway.

"You want me to drive?" I said.

"No, since it's official business, we should probably take mine," the Chief said.

"Bad idea, Chief," Rooster said, shaking his head. "I doubt if they'd do anything stupid, but let's take my truck."

"Something stupid like taking a shot at us?" the Chief said.

"No, they wouldn't do that," Rooster said. "But if they see a police car, they might get spooked and decide to take off and hide in the woods for a while. They know my truck, so that might make it easier."

"Okay," the Chief said, shrugging as he opened the passenger door for me. "Hop in."

"I'll sit in the back," I said, opening the door and climbing in.

Rooster backed down the driveway and headed out of town then charted a route to the Friendly's place using a set of back roads I was vaguely familiar with. I tried to follow along for fifteen minutes, then gave up.

"I can't believe Christmas is in two days," the Chief said. "Where did the year go?"

"What are you getting your wife, Chief?" I said, leaning forward.

"Lots of the usual small stuff she likes," the Chief said, glancing over his shoulder. "But the big one is two tickets to the Cayman Islands."

"You guys decided to come down?" I said. "That's great."

"She doesn't know," the Chief said. "I thought it would be a nice surprise. Are you sure you guys have room for us?"

"Yeah, I'm pretty sure we can squeeze you in," I said, laughing. "When are you coming?"

"Probably late January," he said.

"That's when I'm going," Rooster said. "Maybe we can all go deep sea fishing."

"Count on it," I said. "Rooster is going to stay with my mom."

"You're a brave man," the Chief said, glancing over at Rooster. "How should we play it with these folks?"

"Casual but somber would be my recommendation," Rooster said, turning off the paved road onto a snowy, dirt track that led into the woods. "And try not to use any sudden movements around the son. He can be a little skittish."

"Skittish? Like a horse?" the Chief said.

"Yeah, that's close enough," Rooster said. "Assuming the horse has never been around people before."

The Chief shook his head as he glanced out the window at the woods that were beginning to close in around us. A thick blanket of snow covered the ground, and Rooster's truck bounced along the uneven dirt road. The sunlight disappeared as we got further into the pines and cedars, and I stared out the window at the deep-green trees dappled with white and wondered what would make someone decide to live in the wilderness without any of the modern amenities and creature comforts I took for granted.

On purpose.

The dirt road ended, and Rooster came to a stop in front of a stand of tall pines. I climbed out and looked around at the thick forest that surrounded us on three sides.

"I don't see a house," I said.

"It's a bit of hike from here," Rooster said.

"Great," I said, frowning. "But it is beautiful out here."

"And quiet," the Chief said.

"Good point," Rooster said, motioning at what appeared to be a trail buried in the snow. "We should make some noise going in so they know we're here. It's probably not a good idea to surprise them."

I glanced at the Chief who shrugged as we followed Rooster onto the trail. We walked for what felt like half an hour, then Rooster, noticing the sweat dripping down my face, came to a stop and handed me a bottle of water.

"Thanks," I said, greedily sucking down half the bottle. I handed the rest to Chief Abrams who quickly polished it off.

"Are you okay?" Rooster said, grinning at me.

"This is how these people come and go from home?" I said, breathing heavily.

"Now you understand why they rarely leave," Rooster said, removing another bottle of water from his backpack and taking a long swallow. "Skitch always said his biggest goal in life was just to be left alone."

"Well, mission accomplished," I said, shaking my head. "How much further is it?"

"Just another quarter-mile or so," Rooster said. "By the way, how's your hand?"

"At the moment, it's the least of my concerns."

"We better get going," Rooster said, draining the rest of his water.

He led the way, and we closely followed behind. But after getting smacked in the face a couple of times by pine branches Rooster had pushed his way through, I slipped back and followed at a safe distance. Fifteen minutes later, we came to a stop on the edge of a property that was nothing like I'd expected to see.

A large wooden cabin sat in the middle of what appeared to be about an acre of cleared, fenced land. A barn constructed of the same wood as the cabin and two smaller, stone structures sat nearby. Smoke drifted from two chimneys that were attached at opposite ends of the cabin, and I heard the sounds of a rooster and dozens of chickens that were meandering around inside a fenced pen near the cabin. Inside the pen was an elaborate wooden structure I assumed was a chicken coop.

"It's really nice," I said, stunned.

"Yeah, it certainly is," the Chief said, glancing around. "How much of the land do they own around here?"

"Pretty much all of it," Rooster said, walking toward the cabin.

He stopped when the front door opened and a woman appeared on the porch. She was somewhere in her fifties and hugging a shotgun to her chest with both hands.

"Who goes there?" she called out.

"It's me, Jessie," Rooster said. "Rooster Jennings."

"Hey, Rooster," she said, lowering the gun but continuing to watch us closely. "Come on up."

We followed Rooster up onto the porch, and the woman shook his hand then glanced back and forth at us a few times before leaning the shotgun against the outside wall next to the door.

"Jessie," Rooster said. "This is Chief Abrams from Clay Bay, and this is Suzy Chandler."

"Yeah," she said, nodding. "Nice to meet you. Have a seat." She gestured to a picnic table a few feet away and waited for us to sit down. Then she sat down on the edge of the bench within easy reach of the shotgun. "What are you doing bringing the cops out here, Rooster?"

"We need to talk to you about Skitch," Rooster said.

"What did he do now?" Jessie said.

"He didn't do anything, Jessie," Rooster said as he glanced at the Chief and nodded for him to proceed.

"I'm afraid we have some bad news about your husband, Mrs. Friendly," the Chief said. "He's had an accident."

"An accident?" she said, frowning. "In his truck?"

"No, he had an accident while he was checking his traps yesterday," the Chief said. "I'm so sorry to have to tell you that he's dead."

Jessie sat straight up and stared off into the distance. She was obviously stunned by the news, and I picked up on the expected despair and sadness as well as a healthy dose of confusion. Maybe her thoughts were already on the prospect of having to live out here on her own without her husband's help and companionship. Then, just for an instant, I thought I caught a hint of a smile, and I kicked myself under the table when the thought popped into my head that she might be thinking this was her chance to return to civilization.

It wasn't one of my finest moments, and I continued to chastise myself as I waited for her to respond.

"What happened?" she said after a long silence.

"It looks like he was struck by a stray bullet from a hunter," the Chief said.

"He got shot?" she said, baffled. "That seems pretty unlikely. There couldn't have been more than a handful of people out on the River yesterday."

"The shot came from somewhere off in the distance, and your husband just happened to somehow end up in its path," the Chief said. "He got hit in the shoulder."

"There's no way Skitch was killed by getting shot in the shoulder," Jessie said, shaking her head.

"No, you're right," the Chief said. "But it appears the impact knocked him into the water, and he drowned."

"He drowned?" she said, lowering her head. "I always told him he was crazy spending all that time out there on the River not knowing how to swim."

I sat there pondering the idea that a non-swimmer would spend time on the River by himself but was interrupted when the front door opened and a man and a woman, both around thirty, stepped out onto the porch.

"We have visitors," Jessie said to both of them, then turned back to us. "Would you folks like something to drink?"

"No, I'm good for now, Jessie," Rooster said.

Chief Abrams and I both declined the offer, and the new arrivals sat down at the picnic table. The man stared hard at me. Either his head had managed to grow back into a somewhat normal shape, or his long hair and bushy beard were hiding his malady. His stare flickered with recognition, then he grinned and nodded at me.

"Hey, I know you," he said.

"Hello, Cooter," I said. "How are you doing?"

"Suzy, right?" Cooter said as he did his best bobblehead imitation.

"That's me," I said, giving him a weak smile. "It's been a long time. I'm surprised you remember me."

"You were one of the few folks who was always nice to me," Cooter said.

"I was?" I said, frowning.

"Yeah, remember that time in second grade when I brought that squirrel I shot to Show and Tell?"

"Sure, sure," I said, not having a clue what he was talking about.

"Everybody in class laughed at me," Cooter said, glancing around the table. "And some of the kids even screamed when they saw it. But not Suzy. You know what she said when she saw me with it in the lunchroom?"

"I can't wait to hear this," Rooster whispered.

"Shut it."

"She said that I'd only need a dozen more and then I could make myself a real nice hat," Cooter said, grinning at me.

"Yeah, that sounds like something I'd say," I whispered as I rubbed my forehead.

"Subtle-snarky," Rooster whispered with a grin. "Always one of my personal favorites."

"I said, shut it."

"And you were right. I needed thirteen skins. But I never had a chance to give it to you," Cooter said, hopping up from the table. "Hang on, I'll go see if I can find it."

"He made her a hat?" Chief Abrams whispered to Rooster.

"A *squirrel* hat," Rooster whispered. "I think Cooter's in love."

I kicked Rooster in the shin as I glanced across the table at the woman.

"How are you, Very?" I said, smiling at her.

"I'm good, Suzy," Very Friendly said. "What brings you way out here?"

"Your Papa had an accident," Jessie said. "A bad accident."

"Is he dead?" Very said, her eyes wide.

My neurons flared briefly when she asked if her father was dead. Most people would have probably started off by asking if he was okay. I sat quietly and waited for the mother's response.

"Yes, I'm afraid he is," Jessie said, placing her hand on her daughter's forearm.

I studied Very's reaction to the news about her father. She teared up, then exhaled audibly and looked at her mother.

"How did it happen?" Very said.

"He drowned," Jessie whispered.

"While he was out trapping?"

"Yes," Jessie said.

"Serves him right for treating animals that way," Very eventually whispered with a shrug. "I guess Karma does have a way of catching up with you."

I flinched when I heard her response and glanced over at the mother.

"Those animals are what has fed this family for years," Jessie said, her voice rising a notch.

"They didn't feed me," Very said, flatly.

"Only because you refuse to eat what we put in front of you," Jessie said, then glanced around the table at us. "Very's one of those vegetarians." Then she glared at her daughter. "But that still doesn't give you the right to be rude."

"I wasn't trying to be rude, Mama," Very said without a trace of emotion. "I was merely stating a fact. Papa liked to kill defenseless animals."

"But what about all the other animals you find in the grocery store?" Jessie said. "Weren't they also defenseless?"

"That's the meat-eaters' problem to worry about," Very said.

"Why do I even bother?" Jessie said, staring down at the table.

I frowned at the Chief and Rooster and wondered how the conversation had so quickly transitioned into a debate about dietary choices, but the mother recovered and got us back on course.

"Where is Skitch's body?" she said.

"He's at the funeral home in Clay Bay," Chief Abrams said. "They're waiting for your call to discuss how you'd like to handle the arrangements."

"Well, they're going to be waiting a long time," Jessie said.

"I'm sorry?" the Chief said.

"We ain't got a phone," Jessie said.

"I see," the Chief said, frowning. "Well, I suppose I could give them a message for you."

"Let me check to see if I've got coverage out here," I said, reaching for my phone.

"You won't get any reception here," Very said, getting up from the picnic table. "I think I'm going to take a walk. Would you like to join me, Suzy?"

I looked up at her, then glanced at the Chief.

"You're going to be a while, right?" I said to him.

"Yeah, there are a few things I need to go over with Mrs. Friendly. Go ahead."

"Sure, a walk sounds great," I said, doing my best to sound excited as I forced my feet into action.

I followed Very down the steps, and we walked about a hundred feet until we reached a gate in the fence that surrounded the front yard. Very held it open for me as I walked through, then she led the way through the pines and up a long, sloping incline.

"I can't believe he's dead," Very said, barely above a whisper.

"I'm so sorry for your loss," I said, as always feeling completely inadequate with my response to the grieving. "Were you close?"

"In proximity only," she said, reaching down to grab a pine cone from the snow. She tossed it back and forth in her hands as we continued our walk. "That's about the only thing Papa and I had in common. Can I ask you a question?"

"Sure," I said, following her path over a fallen log.

"Why did you come along with Rooster and the cop?"

"We have your dad's Otterhound," I said, coming to a stop to catch my breath. "At least, we think she was his dog."

"She was. Why would you have Gabby?" Very said, throwing the pine cone into the trees.

"I run an inn for dogs. And my business partner is a vet," I said, pressing a hand against the stitch in my side. "Rooster and I found her at the same time when we discovered your dad's body."

"I see," she said, nodding. "Is she okay?"

Interesting. Is my father dead? Is the dog okay? I tried not to read too much into it.

"She got caught in a trap, and her front left leg is broken," I said.

"That poor dog. One more example of my father's stubbornness," she said. "I tried to tell him it was dangerous to have her around those traps. Whenever Gabby gets focused on a scent, she's relentless."

"I can imagine. But she's going to be fine, and as far as we can tell, all the puppies are okay," I said.

"Puppies?" she said, frowning.

"Yes, Gabby's pregnant."

"How is that possible?" she said, staring at me.

"What?" I said, bewildered by the question.

Then Very laughed and shook her head at me.

"I'm not that much of a bumpkin, Suzy," she said, still laughing. "What I meant to say was that Gabby wasn't supposed to have another litter until next spring."

"Now, I'm really confused," I said, following her as she resumed her casual stroll.

"Papa had her on an annual breeding schedule," Very said.

"Your father was breeding Otterhounds?" I said, stunned.

"Does artificial insemination count as breeding?"

"Yeah, it sure does," I said, nodding.

"Then, yes, he was breeding Otterhounds," Very said as she continued to climb the incline.

"Can we stop for a second?" I said, gasping for breath as a multitude of questions began bouncing around my head.

"Hang on," she said, glancing back at me without slowing down. "We're almost there."

I did my best to hang tough and stay close to her. A few minutes later, we came to the top of the incline where two large tree stumps sat in a clearing about three feet off the ground. I pulled my gloves tight then brushed the snow off one with my good hand and sat down, exhausted. Very sat down on the other stump and glanced around.

"As much as I detest living out here, I have to admit that it's pretty."

"Very," I said, nodding as I looked around.

"Yes?"

"What?"

"Oh, never mind. I thought you were talking to me," she said, giggling. "Don't worry about it. It happens all the time."

"Can I ask you where your father got the Otterhound?" I said, wiping the sweat from my face. "They're pretty rare."

"Oh, I know," Very said. "I've read where there are only about a thousand of them left in the whole world."

"Where on earth would you read that out here?" I said, frowning at her. "No offense."

"With this," she said, reaching into the pocket of her coat and removing a cell phone. "Don't say a word. Nobody knows I have it." She glanced down at her phone and grinned. "Good reception today."

"You have a cell phone?" I said.

"I do," Very said. "But it wasn't easy to pull off. Last year, my mom had a doctor's appointment, and I tagged along. While she was there, I ducked out to the mall next door and got the phone. I even had to rent a post office box just so none of the paperwork would show up in our mail. Believe me, bills for the cell phone and my credit card would be very hard to explain to Papa."

"You have a credit card?"

"Well, I had to have one to get the phone, right?"

"Sure, sure," I said, rubbing my forehead. "Let's get back to the dog for a moment."

"Okay," she said, sliding her phone back into her pocket.

"Where did your dad get the Otterhound?"

"He said it was a gift," Very said. "But I always assumed he stole it. Or maybe traded something for it."

"And he knew how rare Otterhounds are?"

"I'm sure he did," Very said. "He got a lot of money for those puppies."

"Gabby was artificially inseminated?" I said, fighting back against the onset of a headache.

"Yes. Two times over the past couple of years. But if she's pregnant again, I guess that makes three."

"Were you around the first two times she was inseminated?" I said, glancing over at her. She frowned at me and waited until the penny dropped. "Of course, you were. Sorry. Dumb question."

"It wasn't like I watched or anything," she said. "But Papa did tell me what was going on."

"Did anybody show up to give him a hand?" I said, still perplexed.

"No, he handled it by himself," she said, shaking her head. "Cooter was with him in the barn, but I doubt he was much help."

"But where did he get the semen?"

"From a male Otterhound would be my guess," she said, raising an eyebrow at me.

"Funny," I said, laughing.

"Thanks, I'm a little out of practice making small talk."

"You're doing very well," I said. "So, your dad just showed up with the semen?"

"Yes."

"But you don't know where he got his hands on it?"

"Not a clue," she said. "Does it matter?"

"I'm not sure," I said, staring off into the distance as my neurons flared. "Did people show up to buy the puppies?"

"No, we took care of them until they were around seven weeks old, then Papa drove off with them. I just assumed somebody else handled the sales. Nobody has ever been out here to buy a puppy. You saw how hard it is to find the place." Her phone chirped, and she glanced down and smiled. "Oh, I've been waiting for this. Excuse me for a second."

I watched her scroll through the message, then respond, thumbs a blur. She waited for a response, then giggled and sent a short reply back. She slipped the phone back into her pocket.

"He's so bad," she said, her eyes dancing.

"Boyfriend?" I said.

"Not yet," she said, grinning. "We've just texted back and forth so far. But he just confirmed that he's going to take me to dinner. In a real restaurant. Can you believe that?"

"Hey, you gotta eat, right?" I said, shrugging. "Where is he taking you?"

"To some restaurant in Clay Bay called C's," she said, grinning. "Are you familiar with it?"

"Yes, I am. Actually, I'm one of the owners," I said, deciding there was no reason not to divulge that fact. "You'll like it. The chef is amazing."

"I'm dying for a good steak," she said, glancing around as the snow began falling even harder.

"Steak? I thought you were a vegetarian," I said.

"Only around here," she said, scowling. "Have you ever eaten muskrat or squirrel? Or worse, possum?"

"No, I can't say that I have."

"Smart choice," she said. "Venison is okay, and I love chicken, but if I were to eat them in front of everybody, Papa would expect me to eat everything else from the forest he and Cooter killed. My father was pretty adamant about eating what's in front of you, and he considered it *uppity* for me to pick and choose. I got tired of fighting with him about it and came up with the vegetarian thing. It comes in pretty handy."

"Can I ask you a question?"

"Sure."

"How are you going to slip away for your date without being noticed?" I said.

"Easy," she said, shrugging it off. "I'll just tell Mama I'm spending the night out here."

"Out here in the woods? In December?"

"Sure, it's not like it's the middle of winter," she said. "Anytime I get cabin fever and need to get away for a while, I just come out here, put my tent up, and build a fire. And as long as I catch a few fish and bring them back with me the next day, they won't bat an eye." Then she obviously remembered the news about her father and began to tear up. "I mean Mama and Cooter won't bat an eye. Whew, where did that come from? I guess I can't believe Papa's dead."

"You weren't close, were you?"

"Does it show?" she said, dabbing at her eyes with a handkerchief. "No, we tolerated each other. I was the daughter he never wanted. Papa only wanted boys."

"What did you do after he pulled you and Cooter out of school?" I said.

"Cried for about three months, then locked myself in my room for another two," she said, managing a small laugh. "Then I just read and taught myself."

"Really? How did you do that?"

"Once a month, my mother would take me to the town library, and I'd borrow ten, sometimes twenty, books at a time."

"Well, you've obviously done a very good job," I said, impressed by both her demeanor and maturity. "Now that your dad is gone, what are your plans?"

"Try to convince my mother to sell this place and get the heck out of here, what else?" she said, shrugging.

"Will that be difficult?"

"I sure hope not," Very said.

"You could always just leave, right?" I said.

"No, I couldn't leave her by herself out here with Cooter," she said, shaking her head. "That would be cruel."

"I see," I said, impressed by her devotion to her mom. "So, when is this guy taking you out to dinner?"

"The day after Christmas," she said, then pointed out into the distance. "Do you see that path over there?"

"I think so," I said, squinting as I followed her arm.

"That path winds through the back of the property and eventually runs straight into the paved road," Very said. "He's going to pick me up there at six."

"Dress warm," I said, then caught the look she was giving me. "You know, just in case he's late. You don't want to get a chill before your big date."

"My first date," she said, her eyes dancing again.

"Really?"

"Hard to believe, huh?"

"Not considering some of the slumps I've gone through," I said.

"What?"

"Nothing," I said, smiling. "I'm sure you'll have a great time."

"Me too," she said, getting up from the tree stump. "We should probably get back in case my mom needs me."

"Sure," I said, reaching for my phone. "I just need to make one quick call." Josie answered on the second ring. "Hey, it's me."

"How's it going out there?"

"It's...surprisingly good," I said, smiling at Very. "Considering the circumstances."

"Yeah, a death in the family is always tough," Josie said. "Especially the husband and father."

"You're right," I said. "The Otterhound's name is Gabby."

"Cool name."

"How's she doing?"

"Apart from the bad wheel, she's doing pretty good," Josie said. "But I think she could be several days away from delivering."

"Which means we'll have to delay our departure date to Cayman," I said.

"Yeah, probably."

"But that's not a big deal."

"Look, there's no reason for you to stick around," Josie said. "I'll stay here and take care of the delivery and surgery then head down."

"No, I think I'll stay," I said, getting up from the tree stump.

"Are you telling me there's a reason you need to stick around?" she said. "As in, the guy's death might not have been an accident?"

"No, I'm not saying that at all," I said. "I just want to stick around and keep you company."

"And maybe do a little more snooping while you're here?"

"Nothing gets past you."

I put my phone away and walked next to Very as we began our walk down the long incline that led back to the cabin.

"What do you think your mom is going to want to do about Gabby?" I said, finding the walk back much easier.

"Well, since she's pregnant, I imagine she'll want to keep her around for a while."

"For a while?" I said, frowning.

"Mama's not really a dog lover," Very said. "But she knows what those puppies are worth."

"Gabby's going to need surgery on her leg as soon as she delivers," I said.

"That sounds expensive," Very said, scuffing the snow with her boots as she walked.

"Don't worry about that," I said. "We'll figure something out. What about you?"

"What about me?" she said, glancing over at me.

"Are you a dog lover?"

"At first, I wasn't. But now I like having Gabby around," Very said, then recited from memory. "The better I get to know people, the more I find myself loving dogs."

"Somebody famous said that, right?"

"Charles DeGaulle," she said, then chuckled. "Not that I've had much of a chance to get to know people living out here," she said. "Do you know that, apart from my family, you're the first person I've spoken face to face with in almost a year?"

"Well, that's going to change soon, right?" I said, smiling at her. "You've got a big date coming up."

"Yes, I do," she said, nodding. "You got any tips for me?"

"Definitely have the chocolate soufflé."

"Actually, I was talking about ways to make the date extra special," Very said, laughing.

"So was I."

# Chapter 7

I followed Very onto the porch and sat back down at the picnic table between Rooster and the Chief. Between our trek on the way in and my walk with Very through the woods, I was exhausted and my knees and ankles ached. I glanced out at the path that led back to where we'd parked and wondered how much I'd have to pay them to carry me back to Rooster's truck.

"How was your walk?" Chief Abrams said.

"Peachy," I said, reaching for the glass of water that sat in front of him.

"Hang on," Rooster said, trying to grab the glass before I got my hands on it.

"I'm parched," I said, then drained the glass, gagged as my throat seemed to catch fire, and began a massive coughing fit that finally ended just before I hacked up a lung.

"Good, huh?" Rooster said, laughing.

"Smooth," I croaked, wiping my mouth with the back of my glove. "What on earth is that stuff?"

"It's my shine," Jessie said. "Cleans those sinuses right out, doesn't it?"

"At a minimum," I said. "Geez, that's strong."

"You're supposed to sip it," Rooster said, laughing.

"I'll try to remember that," I said, sucking cold air into my lungs. "What do you make it with?"

"Corn and some other grains," Jessie said, deflecting. "It's an old family recipe my great-granddaddy used to use. He's was a bootlegger back during Prohibition."

"You make your own booze?" I said.

"I kinda have to," she said, shrugging. "It's not like I can just run down the street for a six-pack. Besides, it gives me something to do in the winter other than needlepoint."

"Fair enough," I said, my internal organs finally starting to settle down. "Did you speak with Jessie about the dog?"

"No," Rooster said. "We thought we'd wait for you."

"What about the dog?" Jessie said, focusing on me.

"She's got a broken leg," I said. "She got her front left leg caught in one of your husband's traps."

"I tried to tell him not to take that dog with him when he went trapping," Jessie said, shaking her head. "Is she okay?"

"She's going to need surgery," I said.

"How much is that going to cost me?" she said.

"Don't worry about that," I said, waving it away. "But we won't be able to do the surgery until after she delivers her litter."

I watched her reaction closely. Primarily, it was a combination of surprise and confusion.

"Gabby's pregnant?" she said. "That's impossible."

"We think she's about a week away from delivering," I said, shrugging.

Jessie sat quietly, deep in thought. Then she shook her head and looked at me.

"When can I come in and pick her up?"

"She should probably stay with us until she delivers and then has her surgery," I said. "I'm gonna guess at least a couple of weeks."

"Okay," she said, giving it some thought. "But all the puppies are mine, right?"

"Of course," I said, surprised by the question. "We'd never separate you from your dogs."

"No," she said, embarrassed. "Of course, you wouldn't." She perked up and glanced at Rooster and the Chief. "Some more shine, gentlemen?"

"No, thanks," the Chief said. "We should probably get going."

"Yeah, it's starting to come down pretty heavy," Rooster said, getting to his feet. "I'm sorry to have to drop in with bad news like this, Jessie."

She shrugged and sipped her glass of moonshine.

"Do you know what you're going to do now, Jessie?" I said.

"Now, that is a good question," she said, slowly nodding her head. "And I'm going to have to give it some serious thought."

"Well, just let me know if you need anything," Rooster said.

"Thanks, Rooster," she said. "What about Skitch's truck?"

"We'll make sure it gets dropped off," Chief Abrams said.

"Thanks," she said, slipping back into deep thought.

The front door flew open, and Cooter dashed out onto the porch with one hand behind his back.

"Oh, good," he said, excited. "You're still here. Look what I found."

He held a furry object directly in front of my face.

"This is for you," he said, placing it in my hand. "It's the hat I was talking about. I made this for you."

"Gee, thanks, Cooter," I said, slowly turning it over in my hands, half-expecting it to bite me.

"Try it on," he said, bouncing up and down.

"Sure, sure," I said, sliding the hat over my head. It was way too big, and it fell over my ears and covered my forehead.

"Perfect fit," Cooter said. "Do you like it?"

"It's…unbelievable," I said, glancing at Rooster and the Chief who were trying not to laugh.

"Just think of me when you wear it," Cooter said.

"I'm sure I'll have a hard time thinking of anyone else, Cooter," I said, pushing the hat up so I could see. "Thanks. That was very sweet of you."

"I'm glad you like it," he said, bouncing again.

"We should get going," the Chief said. "I'll let you know about the truck, Jessie. And I'll make sure the funeral home gets your instructions."

"Thanks," Jessie said, getting up from the table.

"Again, we're really sorry about what happened to Skitch," Rooster said. "He was a good guy."

"You really think so, Rooster?" Jessie said, frowning at him.

"Well, sure," Rooster said, taken aback. "Cooter, Very, it was nice seeing you. And I'm sorry for your loss."

I waved goodbye and followed Rooster and Chief Abrams down the steps and toward the trail that led back to the truck.

"Man, it's really coming down," the Chief said. "You sure you're going to be able to find your way back to where you parked?"

"Pretty sure," Rooster said. "But not to worry. We've got Davy Crockett here to lead the way."

"Shut it."

"Yeah, nice hat," the Chief said. "And if things don't work out between you and Max, I'm sure Cooter will be more than happy to step up and do some serious *courtin'*."

"Don't be mean," I said, glancing over my shoulder to make sure we were out of sight. I removed the hat and stuffed it into my bag. "It was sweet of him to do that."

"Just make sure you remember to feed it," Rooster said. "You don't want to be walking around with a hungry hat on your head."

"Knock it off," I said, staggering slightly as the effect of the half-glass of moonshine I'd chugged started to kick in. "I'm trying to concentrate."

"Well, then you better put your thinking cap back on," the Chief said.

"Keep it up, and one of you will be getting it as a Christmas present."

That shut them up.

# Chapter 8

I rubbed olive oil and herbs over a large tray of chopped vegetables, added salt and pepper along with a few sprigs of fresh Rosemary, then slid them into the oven. I washed my hands and glanced at Chef Claire who was taking the temperatures of our guests of honor. For the record, our guests were an enormous beef tenderloin, a twenty-pound turkey, and a smoked ham that Rooster had brought along to our annual Christmas Eve dinner.

"Okay," I said, tossing the dish towel over my shoulder. "What's next?"

"I think we're good," Chef Claire said, glancing around the kitchen. "But I wouldn't mind a refill on my wine if you're buying."

"That I can do," I said, refilling her glass. "If you don't need anything else, I'm going to head in."

"I'll just be a few minutes," she said, closing the oven doors.

"Merry Christmas," I said, giving her a hug.

"Same to you," she said, squeezing me tight.

"And there's really no reason for you to stick around," I said. "Josie and I will get down there just as soon as we get things settled with the Otterhound."

"No, I'd like to stay," she said. "Maybe I'll get a few days of cross-country in."

"When you could be hanging out on the beach?"

"I'll have four months to do that," Chef Claire said. "Besides, I'm sure Josie is going to need all the help she can get trying to keep you out of trouble."

"Funny," I said, making a face at her as I headed for the living room.

I spotted my mother and her boyfriend Paulie sitting on one of the couches. Queen, the Cavalier King Charles spaniel we'd given her for her last birthday, was, as always, perched on her lap taking everything in. Directly across from them were Rooster and Chief Abrams. Everyone was sipping eggnog and sampling appetizers from the elaborate collection Chef Claire had put together. My mother slid closer to Paulie as I approached and patted the couch. I sat down and glanced around at our other guests.

"Did you put the dogs downstairs?" I said to Josie as she handed me a glass of eggnog.

"Yeah, it was just too crowded with them here. Between all these people eating and drinking, the tree and the gifts, and eight wagging tails, it was a disaster just waiting to happen," she said, sitting down between Rooster and the Chief. "So, I gave them a snack, a fresh batch of toys, and they're all settled in."

"And how did you escape being banished?" I said to Queen as I scratched her ear.

"I think she's permanently attached to your mom's lap," Paulie said, laughing as he scratched the dog's other ear.

"She's gorgeous," Josie said, beaming at the King Charles.

"So, what's this about the three of you postponing your trip?" my mother said.

"I need to be here to keep an eye on the Otterhound until she delivers," Josie said. "And then I'll do the surgery on her leg."

"And what's your excuse?" my mother said, glancing over at me.

"She'll be Snoopervising," Josie deadpanned.

"Funny," I said. "I'm just going to stick around and give Josie a hand."

"I see," my mother said. "Okay. But that means you won't be in Cayman for my New Year's Eve party."

"Probably not," I said. "Sorry, Mom."

"Just promise me you won't do anything crazy," my mother said.

"What makes you think I would do something crazy?" I said, frowning at her.

"Rhetorical, right?" Josie said to Rooster.

"There's really nothing suspicious about this one," I said. "The guy got shot by a stray bullet then fell into the water and drowned."

"Well done, darling," my mother said, nodding. "I'm so happy when you let the facts speak for themselves."

"I'm impressed," Chief Abrams said.

"Thanks," I said. "Although there is one thing that's bugging me."

A collective groan filled the room.

"Relax," I said. "It's probably not a biggie, but I do have a question for Paulie."

"Me?" Paulie said, frowning. "I don't know anything about Otterhounds and even less about muskrat trapping."

"Which should make her next question highly entertaining," the Chief said, laughing.

"I'm seeing your name on a wonderful gift," I said, raising an eyebrow at him.

Rooster snorted.

"Okay," Paulie said. "What's your question?"

"What do you know about dog semen?"

"I beg your pardon?" Paulie said, baffled.

"Not regular dog semen," I said. "Illegal semen."

"Wow," he said, glancing at my mother. "I wouldn't have gotten that with a million guesses."

"Me either," my mother said, staring at me. "Darling, must you? It's Christmas Eve. Just tell your neurons that if they don't behave, Santa won't come."

Josie and Rooster burst out laughing.

"You two are no help at all," I said, glaring at both of them.

"Yeah, we're the problem here," Josie said, shaking her head. "But please continue. You definitely have my attention."

"Don't encourage her," my mother said.

"I'm just wondering if Paulie, back when he was working on the dark side, ever happened to come across any criminals who were involved in high-end dog breeding."

"Why on earth would you ask that question?" my mother said, stroking Queen's head.

"I'm just confused about something," I said, frowning. "How would a guy who lived in the wilderness end up owning a rare Otterhound and then start breeding it via artificial insemination?"

"He was breeding the Otterhound?" Josie said, surprised by the news.

"Yes, according to Very," I said. "She said her dad had used AI for two previous litters but wasn't planning on the next one until sometime in the spring."

"He must have changed his mind," Josie said. "Was he selling the puppies?"

"Not individually. Very said he would sell the whole litter off when they were around seven weeks. She also said she doesn't know where he got the semen or who he was selling the puppies to."

"How much money is involved in something like that?" my mother said.

"Well, since Otterhounds are pretty rare, you could probably get up to three grand each," Josie said. "Maybe more. And an average litter is somewhere around six puppies."

"But Skitch wouldn't have gotten all that money," Rooster said. "He was probably paid a fee for the litter. He might have got five grand if he was lucky."

"But for somebody who lived the way that family does, five grand would be a lot of money, right?" I said.

"Yeah, I imagine it would," Rooster said, nodding. "But it's just such a weird thing for Skitch to be involved in."

"Have you ever come across anything like that before?" I said to Paulie.

"No, that's a new one on me," he said, shaking his head. "But if you were dealing with rare breeds and producing lots of litters, I guess it's enough money to make it worth the effort."

"Would it be possible for you to make a few calls?" I said.

"And do what?" he said, laughing. "See if any of my old buddies know where I can buy a rare dog?"

"Not just a rare dog," I said. "An Otterhound puppy."

"You're joking, right?" Paulie said, staring at me. Then he turned to my mother. "She's joking, isn't she?"

"Take a good look at her face," my mother said.

"Okay, now I see it," Paulie said, staring at me. "She's not joking. Suzy, I wouldn't know where to start."

"C'mon, Paulie," I said. "Please."

"Don't beg, darling. It's most unbecoming."

"Just a couple of calls," I said. "Somebody in your former circle must know who might be involved in something like that."

"I don't know, Suzy," Paulie said. "Why do you even want to know?"

"I just have a nagging feeling that it's somehow important," I said.

"Important how?" the Chief said.

"I don't know," I said, frowning. "And that's what is driving me nuts."

"Maybe somebody in the family was trying to pull a fast one on Friendly," Josie said.

"Now, that's interesting," I said, nodding.

"Well, there goes our last chance for a quiet dinner," my mother said, glaring at Josie. "You're as bad as she is."

"No, think about it, Mrs. C.," Josie said. "Maybe the kids decided they wanted to get some of that money. Somehow they managed to get their hands on some illegal semen and impregnate the dog without their father knowing anything about it."

"How would they keep a litter of puppies a secret for almost two months?" the Chief said.

"Now, that is a very good question," Josie said, sipping eggnog. "Never mind."

"No, hang on," I said, giving it some thought before discarding the idea. Then I shook my head. "No, you're right. That would be really tough to do." My neurons flared, and I glanced around with a smile. "Unless they took the dog off the property before she gave birth."

"There you go," Josie said, grinning. "That's our girl."

"But Very said she didn't know the dog was pregnant," I said. "She seemed genuinely surprised when I told her. And so did the mother now that I think about it."

"Then maybe it was the son," Josie said. "Old, what's his name."

"Cooter?" Rooster said. "I doubt it. That guy couldn't pull something like that off if you spotted him the puppies, the truck, and a roadmap."

"How did his head turn out?" my mother said.

"It's hard to tell. It's pretty much hidden by his hair and beard," Rooster said.

"That's probably a good call," my mother said, then again pressed the tips of her fingers together. "It was so *smushed*. What's he up to these days?"

"He's a budding milliner," Rooster said, grinning at me.

"He makes women's hats?" my mother said, frowning.

"He does," the Chief said, nodding. "And we've seen some of his work."

"Really?" my mother said. "What's it like?"

"I'm gonna go with…memorable," the Chief deadpanned.

"Don't forget furry," Rooster said.

"No, we can't forget that," the Chief said. "I sort of liked it, but I imagine some people would consider it downright squirrelly."

"Are you guys done?" I said, glaring at them before I refocused on Paulie. "What do you say?"

"Okay," Paulie said. "I'll make a few calls just for the giggles. But if I end up with an Otterhound puppy, you're on the hook for the three grand."

"Deal," I said, settling into the couch with a huge smile.

# Chapter 9

I woke early the next morning, and my Christmas began with me taking our house dogs outside so they could take care of business before they opened their presents. But not until I'd put a big pot of coffee on to brew. It was cold, but not brutal, and a light snow was falling, the perfect weather for Christmas Day. I called my boyfriend, Max, a disaster relief consultant who was currently in Columbia helping people dig out from a massive landslide that had happened four days earlier. He answered on the third ring.

"Hey," he said. "Merry Christmas."

"Merry Christmas," I said, exhaling audibly when I remembered how much I missed having him here for the holidays. "What are you doing?"

"Well, at the moment," Max said. "I'm talking with a couple of the engineers, and we're trying to decide if there is any way we can get a backhoe in here or whether we're going to have to recruit several hundred people with shovels."

"How bad is it?" I said, watching as Captain and Chloe started wrestling in the snow. Then Al and Dente joined in, and soon all four dogs were rolling around and kicking snow in every direction.

"The property damage is heartbreaking," Max said. "But it looks like we might have gotten lucky getting all the people out."

"That's good," I said. "I wish you were here."

"Me too," Max said. "But I should be out of here in a week, ten days tops, and I'll be heading straight to Grand Cayman."

"I can't wait."

"What are you guys doing today?"

"Coffee, then the dogs will be opening their presents, breakfast, open our presents, and then we'll head over to my mom's place for lunch. After that, we'll stop by some friends' places to drop off some gifts and then come home to change into our pajamas and relax in front of the fire."

"Organized," Max said, laughing.

"Yeah, over the years we've refined our game plan," I said, then noticed that Chloe had one of Captain's ears in her mouth and was tugging hard. "Chloe, you're just asking for trouble."

"Look, I'm going to need to run," Max said. "But I'll call you later on after things settle down a bit here."

"Okay," I said. "I'll just bring all your gifts with me to Cayman, and we'll open them down there."

"You read my mind," he said. "Wish everyone a Merry Christmas for me, and I'll talk with you later."

"Will do," I said.

"I love you, Suzy."

"Love you, too."

I slid the phone back into my coat pocket and whistled. All four dogs, covered in snow, stopped wrestling and cocked their heads at me.

"Snack?" I said, walking toward the house.

The dogs easily beat me to the kitchen door and waited impatiently for me to climb the steps.

"Shake," I said, glancing around at all four. "Shake."

Eventually, they all complied, and I opened the door. Chef Claire and Josie were up and sipping coffee in their robes. We exchanged hugs and holiday greetings, then I grabbed a jar of the jerky that Chef Claire had made for the dogs. I gave all four of them way too much, then they headed into the living room to stretch out in front of the fire that was already roaring.

"You spoil them," Josie said, nodding at the jar of jerky.

"It's Christmas," I said, sitting down at the kitchen island. "Max said to say Merry Christmas."

"How's he doing?" Chef Claire said.

"He sounded good," I said. "But he misses me."

"He better," Josie said, laughing. "Who's turn is it to cook Christmas breakfast?"

"I think it's mine," Chef Claire said. "French toast, pancakes, or omelet?"

Josie glanced at me as I thought about the options. There wasn't a bad choice among them, and I eventually shrugged.

"French toast," Josie said.

"Good call," I said as my phone chirped. I checked the number, then put the phone on speaker and answered. "Merry Christmas, Paulie."

"Same to you," he said. "Is everybody there?"

"We are," Chef Claire said. "Merry Christmas."

"Merry Christmas, guys," he said. "Your mom wanted me to check to see what time you're coming over."

"No later than noon," I said. "What's she making for lunch?"

I'm very big on the true meaning of Christmas, and I love giving and receiving gifts, but I'm also a devotee of Christmas Day menus. And my mother always went all out for the annual lunch she served to us and several of her close friends.

"She's doing a stuffed pork tenderloin and some Swedish potato dish," Paulie said. "From what she says, it sounds like they're a hassle."

"Not a hassle," Chef Claire said, laughing. "Hasselback."

"She's making Hasselback potatoes?" Josie said, softly clapping her hands. Then she turned to Chef Claire. "Did you give her your recipe?"

"I did," Chef Claire said. "Yum. That sounds great."

"It certainly does," I said, my stomach gurgling. "Just tell her we'll be there in plenty of time for lunch. We'll see you in a bit, Paulie."

"Hang on," he said. "I have some news for you."

"Already?" I said, frowning.

"Yeah, I had to call some friends this morning to wish them a Merry Christmas, so I decided I might as well ask a few questions," he said, then laughed. "And I figured it was a good way to keep you from nagging me about it all day."

"Funny," I said, making a face at the phone. "Did you find anything out?"

"Actually, I did," Paulie said. "Apparently, there is a rather active black market for rare dogs. Who knew, huh?"

"Who did you talk to?"

"Gino the Jet," Paulie said. "But everybody calls him Greasy Fingers."

"But not because he eats a lot of fried food, right?" I said, laughing.

"Nothing gets past you," he said. "Anyway, he told me that he recently bought a dog called a Volpino Italiano."

"Sure," Josie said, nodding as she sipped her coffee. "The Italian Spitz."

"Yeah, that rings a bell," I said. "But I don't think I've ever seen one before. They're a little fur ball, right? Looks a lot like a Pomeranian?"

"Yes. And they're very rare," Josie said. "Especially outside of Italy."

"That's where Gino got the idea," Paulie said. "He took his family to Rome last year, and a relative had one of those dogs. He went nuts over it and just had to have one."

"And this black market just happened to have puppies available?" I said, frowning.

"No, it was a lot more involved than that," Paulie said. "It took several months, and the whole process ended up costing him close to twenty grand."

"It probably would have been cheaper just to move to Italy," Josie said, shaking her head.

"Does this Gino know who's behind the operation?" I said.

"I'm sure he does," Paulie said. "But he declined to say."

"Well, that's not a lot of help," I said, deflated.

"But he did give me the name of the woman who manages it," Paulie said. "I told Gino I was looking for an Otterhound puppy and needed to get in touch with somebody who might be able to help me out."

"You're so good," I said. "When are you going to call them?"

"I've already done it," Paulie said. "In fact, I just got off the phone with her. Her name's Sofia Rossi."

"You called her on Christmas?" I said.

"Why not? It was just a phone call. It's not like I tried to climb down her chimney."

"Fair enough," I said, shaking my head at his logic. "Where does she live?"

"That's the interesting part," Paulie said. "She has a place just outside Cape Vincent."

"Wow," I said, nodding. "That's close."

"There's somebody running a black market breeding operation around here?" Josie said, frowning.

"Apparently," Paulie said.

"Why haven't we heard anything about it?" Josie said.

"I doubt if they talk about it much or run ads, and I imagine they don't sell the dogs around here," he said. "She was pretty cautious at first, but after I told her that Gino had given me her name, she opened up."

"What did she have to say about Otterhounds?" I said.

"She said she is expecting to have a litter sometime in the spring," he said.

"That was the timeframe that Very mentioned," I said. "But if her dad had moved the date up, surely the woman handling the puppies would know that."

"One would think," Paulie said.

"Maybe somebody was trying to do an end-run around both Friendly and the woman," Josie said.

"But that would mean they'd have to get their hands on the semen and then somehow manage to impregnate the Otterhound," I said. "It has to be somebody inside the family, right?"

"That's the only thing that makes any sense," Josie said. "Not that any of it makes much sense."

"Did she quote you a price?" I said to Paulie.

"Five grand," he said.

"Geez," I said, grimacing. "That's a lot of money. Where did you leave it with her?"

"I told her I was going out of town, but one of my representatives would be getting in touch with her soon," Paulie said.

"Your representative by the name of Suzy, right?" I said.

"You are on fire today," he said. "Look, I gotta run. Your mother wants to show me the new bathing suit she bought."

"Oh, that's right," I said. "You guys are flying out in a couple of days."

"We are," Paulie said. "And I can't wait."

"Thanks so much, Paulie," I said. "I owe you big time. We'll see you in a while. And remember, no matter what it looks like, you *love* the new bathing suit."

"Do I look like an idiot?" he said, laughing. "Later."

I ended the call and glanced back and forth at Josie and Chef Claire.

"That was way too easy," I said, grinning. "I've got a great idea. Who feels like doing a little Otterhound shopping tomorrow?"

"I think I'll pass," Josie said. "I'll stay here just in case I need to do a little Otterhound *delivery*."

"Sure," I said. "How about you?"

"No, I've got some stuff to handle at the restaurant," Chef Claire said.

"Like what?"

"I'm sure I'll think of something," Chef Claire said, grinning at me. "And I'm going cross-country skiing with Freddie."

"When did you organize that?" I said.

"Just as soon as I can call him," Chef Claire said, laughing.

"Fine," I said, frowning. "You're gonna miss all the fun."

Josie glanced at Chef Claire who shook her head.

"We must have a different definition of fun," Chef Claire said.

"That must be it," Josie said. "How about we have the dogs open their presents? Then we can eat."

"Now, that's what a great idea sounds like," Chef Claire said, beaming at me.

# Chapter 10

The next morning Sofia Rossi told me over the phone that she was attending a memorial service and couldn't meet with me about the Otterhound puppy until tomorrow. My neurons flared when she mentioned the memorial service, and I immediately called Rooster and confirmed that a service for Skitch Friendly was being held later in the day at our local Catholic church. I debated about tagging along with him and my mother but finally decided against it since my behavior in church the last two times I'd been there had been, as my mother put it, deplorably unladylike.

At least that's what she called it after she'd calmed down. At first, her critique of my performances had been liberally sprinkled with a rather creative combination of expletives I'll avoid repeating here.

Skitch Friendly's death had officially been ruled an accident, and for the moment, I was willing to go along with the prevailing opinion. There was certainly no evidence to suggest foul play as long as one bought the *stray bullet* theory, and hunting accidents weren't that uncommon. But if the recluse's death hadn't been an accident, I was almost certain that it was somehow connected to the mysterious dog breeding operation. And since I already had a plan in place to do some serious snooping in that regard, I opted against attending a memorial service for someone I never knew.

Besides, if I did show up, Cooter would undoubtedly wonder why I wasn't wearing the hat.

I did the breakfast dishes with the assistance of all four dogs who were sitting at my feet and staring up at me like they hadn't eaten in a week. I finally relented and grabbed the jar of jerky from the shelf.

"You're such a soft touch," Chef Claire said as she entered the kitchen and poured herself a cup of coffee.

"They wore me down," I said, laughing. "That outfit looks great."

"I love it," she said, glancing down at the one-piece thermal bodysuit I'd given her for Christmas. "It's tight, but it stretches whenever I move around. It's perfect for cross-country."

"You're going to give Freddie a heart attack," I said, grinning at her.

"Storefront mannequins give Freddie a heart attack," she said, shrugging. "I thought I'd take the dogs with me."

"Great," I said. "They'll love that."

"You sure you don't want to come along?"

I cocked my head and gave her a blank stare.

"Got it," she said. "Dumb question."

"Have fun," I said. "I'll see you at the restaurant later."

"You're coming to C's tonight?" she said, frowning. "Suzy, we've got more leftovers here than we know what to do with."

"Not to eat. I just want to get a look at a couple of your dinner guests."

"Should I even ask?"

"No, I'll explain it all later."

"I'm sure you'll try," Chef Claire said.

Then she herded the dogs outside and followed them carrying her skis and poles. I waved to Freddie who was heading up the driveway, then I watched them disappear into the woods behind the house with the dogs leading the way. I walked down the path to the Inn and entered through the back door and found Josie sitting in the Otterhound's condo and holding her stethoscope against the dog's stomach.

"How's she doing today?" I said, sitting down next to her and stroking the dog's head.

"She's good," Josie said, removing the stethoscope from her ears and sliding it into her lab coat. "But I'm still only getting five heartbeats."

"There's still a chance that you just can't hear the other one, right?"

"There is," Josie said. "But don't get your hopes up."

"She has to be getting close to delivering," I said.

"Yeah, it shouldn't be long," Josie said. "And that's good because her leg is still hurting."

"Are you going to have to rebreak the leg to do the surgery?"

"Oh, I sure hope not," she said. "But if she goes much longer, the bone might start reattaching itself at a weird angle."

"The poor girl," I said, running my hand along the dog's back.

"Yeah, she's been through a lot," Josie said. "I wish I could just do the surgery, but I'm not going to take the chance with the puppies."

"Yeah, I know," I said. "There's a memorial service for Skitch Friendly today."

"Interesting. I wonder if anybody from the family will swing by at some point to check on Gabby," Josie said.

"Great minds think alike," I said. "I know we would if it were our dog."

"We'd be living here if it were our dog," Josie said, laughing.

"Sofia Rossi is going to the memorial service," I said.

"I guess that confirms she was working with Friendly producing the Otterhound litters."

"Yeah, I'm pretty sure it does. I'm going to meet with her tomorrow."

We glanced up when Sammy entered the condo area from registration.

"Good morning," Sammy said to me.

"How are you doing, Sammy?"

"I'm great," he said, kneeling down in front of the Otterhound. "How's our girl doing?"

"She's hanging in there," Josie said.

"I thought I'd take her out to do her business and then get her back in before I let the rest of the dogs out," he said. "You know, just so she's not tempted to join in the horseplay."

"Good idea," Josie said, getting to her feet. "You want to go outside, Gabby?"

The Otterhound climbed to her feet and wagged her tail. Sammy opened the door that faced the dog's play area and bent down to go through it. He called the dog, and she slowly limped her way outside.

"That just breaks my heart," I said, glancing outside.

"She's going to be fine," Josie said. "Did Chef Claire decide to go skiing?"

"Her and Freddie just headed out. She took the dogs with her."

"She's a brave woman," Josie said, shaking her head.

"And she's wearing the outfit I gave her," I said.

"Nice. How does it look?"

"Fantastic," I said. "But it's really skintight."

"Freddie's going to be stepping all over his skis," Josie said, laughing. "Leftovers tonight?"

"Yeah," I said. "But let's eat early. I need to get to the restaurant."

"For what?"

"I just want to take a look at who Very Friendly is having dinner with. It's her first date."

"So, you're going to do some snooping."

"Yeah."

"And there's no sense doing it on an empty stomach, right?"

"I knew you'd understand."

# Chapter 11

I entered C's through the kitchen at six-thirty sharp and glanced around. Given the time of year, the restaurant was staffed with a skeleton crew that consisted of a dishwasher, two wait staff, and Charlie, Chef Claire's sous chef who would be running the kitchen while we were in Cayman. She was chatting and laughing with him and waved when she saw me come in.

"Hey," I said. "How was skiing?"

"It was great," Chef Claire said. "Are the dogs still sacked out?"

"They haven't moved from in front of the fire since they got home," I said. "Hey, Charlie. How are you doing?"

"Things are good," he said, pushing his chef's hat back. "We were just talking about the best way to kill some time."

"It's really dead," Chef Claire said.

"You know, I've always wondered why you guys even keep the place open in the winter," Charlie said.

"It was just something we decided to do," I said, shrugging. "Actually, it was my mother's idea."

"Well, I think it's a nice thing to do for the folks in town, but you guys must lose your shirt during the winter."

"We've got lots of shirts," I said, waving it off.

Charlie, bemused, shook his head and checked the status of some steaks under the broiler.

"You don't mind if I do a little snooping from here in the kitchen, do you?"

"Knock yourself out," Chef Claire said, prepping a dinner plate. "Who's the lucky victim tonight?"

"Very Friendly," I said, stepping back to give one of the wait staff room to hand Chef Claire an order. "Hey, Margot. How was your Christmas?"

"It was great," she said. "And yours?"

"Almost perfect," I said. "But Max is in Columbia and couldn't make it."

"That's too bad," Margot said. "You guys aren't going to believe the woman in the dining room."

"What's she doing?" Chef Claire said.

"Nothing really," Margot said. "It's like she's a three-year-old at Christmas. Bouncing around in her chair, staring wide-eyed at everything. You'd think she'd never been in a restaurant before."

"She hasn't," I said, heading for the two swinging doors that separated the kitchen from the dining room.

"Really?" Margot said.

"Yeah, she doesn't get out much."

I glanced through a porthole window into the dining room and saw Very Friendly at a table with a man who had his back to me.

"Suzy," Chef Claire said. "You need to move."

"I'll just be a second," I said, glancing over my shoulder at her. Then the door swung inward and smacked me hard in the face. I dropped to my knees like I'd been punched.

"Oh, Suzy," Audrey, our other server, said. "I'm so sorry. Are you okay?"

"Not again. Suzy, that's the door people use to come *into* the kitchen. The one on your right is the door to go out," Chef Claire said, scolding me as she walked over. "How many times do I have to tell you?"

"Obviously at least one more than you did," I said, holding a hand to my nose. "Geez, that hurts."

"You're bleeding," Chef Claire said, shaking her head. She grabbed a clean dish towel, rinsed it in warm water and pressed it against my nose. "I can't take you anywhere. Tilt your head back."

I did, and soon my nosebleed stopped. I dabbed the towel against my nose, then washed my face. I tossed the bloody towel in a bin, then slowly opened the out-door and stepped into the dining room. I headed straight for Very's table, and when she saw me, she started waving.

"Suzy," she said. "I was wondering if I'd see you here."

"Hi, Very," I said, still waiting to get a look at her date. "Welcome to C's."

"What happened to your face?" she said, frowning.

"A door bit me," I said, then flinched when I saw who she was with. "You?"

"It's nice to see you, too, Ms. Chandler," Herman Billows, the representative from 3E, said, frowning as he glanced up at me.

My neurons surged as several questions began to bounce around in my head.

"I'm sorry," I said, unable to get the frown off my face. "It's just that when Very told me she was coming here for dinner, I didn't expect to see you."

"Isn't he cute?" Very said, grabbing Herman Billows' hand.

"Sure, sure," I said, glancing back and forth at them. "How did you two meet?"

"He reached out to me via a text message, and then we just started chatting," Very said, squeezing his hand.

"It was pure kismet," Herman said, wincing as he gently extracted his hand to grab his water glass. "We just hit it off. Imagine my surprise when Very told me she'd never been on a date before."

"But here we are," Very said. "You have a beautiful place."

"Thanks," I said, rubbing my forehead. "Look, I need to take care of a few things, but I'll swing by later. And make sure you order dessert. It's on me."

"That's wonderful," Very said. "Isn't that sweet of her, Herman?"

"Very."

"What?"

"No, I meant it was very sweet of her to do that," Herman said, forcing a smile.

"Oh, of course," Very said, giggling.

"Enjoy your dinner," I said. "I'll see you later."

I headed for the lounge that was nearly empty and sat down at the bar. Millie, our head bartender, approached and frowned at my face.

"Did you get hit by the kitchen door again?" Millie said.

"Yeah, I really need to start working on that," I said. "Can I get a glass of Pinot, please?"

Millie poured and placed the glass in front of me. I took a sip, deep in thought. I grabbed my phone and called my mother.

"Hello, darling."

"Hi, Mom. I'm at C's, and I think something weird is going on," I said, taking another sip of wine.

"I'm going to need a bit more," she said. "Our definitions of weird are quite different."

"Do you still have the information your friend in Albany sent you about that vein of natural gas they've found up here?"

"I do," she said. "Why?"

"Because Very Friendly is here at the restaurant on her first ever date."

"Keep talking," my mother said, laughing. "Maybe those two thoughts will collide at some point.

"You'll never guess who she's here with."

"I'm too tired to play twenty questions, darling."

"Herman Billows."

I waited out a long silence.

"Interesting," she whispered.

"I'm gonna stick with weird."

"Hang on a sec," she said.

I heard the rustle of paper, then the sound of her desk chair as she sat down.

"Do you have a map of the area in front of you?" I said.

"I do," she said.

"The Friendly's property has natural gas under it, doesn't it?"

"It sits right in the middle of the vein," she said. "In fact, the whole property is surrounded by it."

"Do you know if Billows spoke to Skitch Friendly before he died?"

"I do not," she said, drumming her fingers on the desk.

"But if he did, is there any chance that Friendly would have agreed to lease his land?" I said, gently rubbing my throbbing nose with my good hand.

"I seriously doubt it," she said. "The last thing he would have wanted is a bunch of wells and people wandering all over his land. And he obviously wasn't very interested in money."

"But now that he's gone, Billows might get a different answer from his wife or kids, right?"

"You tell me," my mother said. "You've seen the place. Would you live out there with none of the basic amenities?"

"Not a chance," I said. "And Very has made it clear she'd like to get out of there. How much money would they be looking at?"

"Certainly enough to move if they wanted. This is not good."

"Does your land along with Rooster's and the Friendly's pretty much cover the area where they've found the deposit?"

"It does," she said. "But from what I'm looking at, the Friendly's land is the centerpiece. If Mr. Billows got his hands on it, they'd be able to sink dozens of wells. I need to call Rooster."

"Okay," I said.

"How long are you going to be there?"

"Long enough to get some answers," I said.

"We'll be there in about half an hour," my mother said, then hung up.

I set my phone on the bar and finished my wine. Millie approached and refilled my glass.

"Thanks."

"Is there a problem?" she said, studying me closely.

"Yeah, I think there might be."

## Chapter 12

I left my second glass of wine untouched and headed back to the dining room. Very was sitting by herself and staring around the room with a huge smile on her face.

"Where's Herman?"

"He had to take a phone call," Very said. "Have a seat and keep me company."

I sat down and tried to formulate an opening question.

"What happened to your hand?" she said.

"Gabby bit me the day we rescued her," I said, glancing down at the fresh bandage Josie had applied earlier today. "Nineteen stitches."

"Really?" Very said, frowning. "I don't think she's ever done that before."

"She was just scared," I said. "She's actually a sweetheart."

"Yeah, I guess she is," Very whispered.

"What's the matter?"

"I was always a bit jealous of all the attention my father gave her. We stopped by your place after the memorial service today."

"Yes, Josie told me," I said. "Your mom is concerned about the puppies."

"I'm sure she is," Very said, shrugging. "There's a lot of money sitting inside that dog at the moment."

"But you didn't know your dad had moved the breeding schedule up?"

"I didn't have a clue," she said, shaking her head.

"So, how was the memorial service?"

"Quiet. Somber," she said. "Not many people showed up. Mama said a few words, then Rooster did a quick tribute. That was about it."

"I'm really sorry about your dad," I said.

"Yeah, for all his craziness and rules, he was a pretty good guy once you got to know him," Very said with a sad sigh. "You're surprised to see me here with Herman, aren't you?"

"Actually, I'm shocked," I said. "Small world, huh?"

"Is that your way of getting to the important topic, Suzy?" Very said, grinning at me.

"You know, Very, for a woman who's spent her life living in the middle of the woods, you're sharp as a tack."

"Thank you."

"So, has Herman floated the idea of leasing your land?"

"He has," Very said. "He mentioned it just after we sat down."

"That was quick," I said.

"He said he wanted to get it out of the way before we got to the really important business," she said.

"Which would be you and him, right?"

"Of course," Very said, laughing. "He thinks he's so smooth. And I imagine his approach does work with a lot of women."

"But not you?"

"I haven't decided yet," Very said. "I want my first boyfriend to be special. And he certainly can take me places and show me things I've only dreamt about."

"I'm waiting for the but," I said.

"Oh, you caught that. *But* it's pretty clear that he's primarily interested in leasing our land," she said. "And Papa always told me that if a man wasn't willing to make me his number one priority, I should run for the hills."

"That's pretty good advice," I said.

"Do as I say, not as I do," she said, shaking her head. "And it's not like I ever had a chance to test out his theory. But it looks like that might be changing."

"Do you think you can get your mother to agree to the lease?"

"I'd be shocked if she didn't," Very said. "She's had a hard life, and without Papa around it's going to get even harder."

"I imagine it is," I said. "Where would you go?"

"I'm pretty sure I can talk Mama into moving to someplace warm," she said. "I don't have to tell you what the winters are like around here. Especially when you're stuck out there."

"No, you don't," I said. "But what about Cooter?"

"Oh, Cooter will never leave," she said, shaking her head. "As long as he can spend his time hunting and fishing, he won't care if there's a gas well parked in the barn."

"The fracking process can be very damaging to the environment," I said. "Especially the River."

"Yes, I've been reading about it," she said.

"And?"

"And it's definitely something to consider," she said.

"As is the money, right?"

"I imagine you and I look at money a bit differently, Suzy," she said, raising an eyebrow at me. "Since you have a lot of it, and I don't have any."

"Fair point," I said, nodding. "And your family is definitely sitting on something that a lot of people would love to get their hands on. Did Herman get a chance to speak with your father before he died?"

"He did," Very said. "But Papa told Herman to get lost almost before he could even explain what he wanted to talk about."

"So, your dad did turn him down?"

"In no uncertain terms."

"I'm so sorry, Very," Herman said, approaching the table. "That call took way too long."

"Don't worry about it," Very said. "Suzy and I are having a nice chat."

"I hope she hasn't been filling your head with stories about what a horrible person I am," Herman said, grinning. "You know, one of those corporate charlatans."

"No, she didn't need to do that," Very said, casually.

Herman Billows flinched, and I hid my smile. Good for you, girl. I glanced over my shoulder when I heard Margot arrive with their dinners. I got up and glanced at their plates.

"You both went with the ribeye," I said. "Good call. Enjoy your dinner. And if you're thinking about the soufflé, you should order them now."

I headed back into the lounge and sat down in the same seat at the bar. Millie slid the glass of wine I hadn't touched back in front of me, and I took a sip. I noticed Millie smiling and waving, and looked over my shoulder and saw my mother and Rooster approaching the bar. I got up to greet them, and we headed toward the fireplace and sat down.

"Are they still here?" my mother said, glancing into the dining room.

"They are," I said. "They just started their entrees."

"Did you get a chance to talk to Very?" Rooster said, holding two fingers up at Millie.

"I did. Billows stepped out to take a call, so I had about ten minutes alone with her."

"And?" my mother said.

"She's more than ready to do the deal," I said. "And she's convinced she can get her mother to sign off as well. Wants to move somewhere warm."

"Can't blame her for that," Rooster said. "What about Cooter?"

"She says there's no way he would ever leave the place," I said. "Which would work out perfectly for Very and her mom. Cooter would be in his element, and they'd have someone taking care of the place while they're off walking the beach."

Millie arrived carrying two steaming snifters of B&B and set them down in front of my mother and Rooster.

"Thanks, Millie," my mother said, beaming up at her before refocusing on me. "Did she mention any specifics about what Billows is offering?"

"No, I don't think they've gotten that far," I said. "But Very said he brought it up right after they'd sat down tonight."

"Billows is about as subtle as a truck, huh?" Rooster said.

"He told her that he wanted to get business out of the way so they could focus on the important stuff. Like their relationship."

"He's trying to take advantage of that poor girl's background?" my mother said, frowning. "The little weasel."

"That was my first thought. But Very's already got him pegged," I said. "It's strange, but she's incredibly worldly for someone who's spent her life living in the woods."

"Did she say anything else?" Rooster said.

"Billows talked to her dad about the lease rights before he died," I said, glancing back and forth at them.

"But Billows didn't get anywhere, did he?" Rooster said.

"No, Very's dad sent him packing straight away," I said, grimacing as I felt the onset of a headache. "You don't think Billows might have been involved in his death, do you?"

"Take Skitch out, then swoop in and try to get to the mother through Very?" Rooster said, frowning. "That's a bit of a stretch."

"Especially for lease rights in an area where there's a drilling ban in effect," my mother said.

"How close is the State to reversing its decision on fracking?" I said.

"According to my friends in Albany, not close at all," she said. "But there's constant noise coming from the lobbyists. And we're always only one election cycle away from potential disaster."

"Now, that's a cheery thought," I said, laughing.

"You asked," my mother said, shrugging.

"I guess there's only one thing left to do," Rooster said.

"Absolutely," my mother said, nodding as she took a sip of her drink.

"What's that?" I said.

"Pay Jessie Friendly another visit," Rooster said.

"What for?"

"To make her an offer on the property," my mother said.

I thought about it for a moment then nodded.

"Yeah. That could work."

# Chapter 13

For the first time since Rooster and I had discovered the body of Skitch Friendly, my neurons had turned relentless and were beginning to torment me with the idea that his death hadn't been accidental. But without a clear motive or any probable suspects, that notion remained a neuron-induced annoyance. Rooster was right. The possibility that Herman Billows might have been directly involved in Friendly's death was definitely a stretch. However, if Billows future with his company was somehow tied to his ability to secure lease rights in our neck of the woods, and if he turned out to be someone who didn't like hearing no for an answer, I could definitely connect the dots back to him.

But it was another possible motive that was nagging at me this morning during the twenty-mile drive to Sofia Rossi's farm just outside of Cape Vincent. The thought that Friendly's death was somehow related to the breeding and sale of rare dogs had forced its way into my head late last night and kept me awake until around three when I finally dozed off and dreamt of being chased through a frigid marsh by a rabid Otterhound wearing a squirrel hat. And as I stumbled through the decayed cattails, occasionally losing my footing and sliding into the freezing water, I woke myself up when I wondered aloud if the

Otterhound had wanted to bite me or was merely trying to give me the hat back.

It wasn't the strangest dream I'd ever had.

But it was a lot like it.

The drive to Cape Vincent should have a been leisurely half-hour trip where I'd be able to enjoy River views, but it was, again, snowing hard and I white-knuckled my way along Route 12 doing thirty miles an hour over close to half a foot of unplowed accumulation. As such, my drive to the small, but gorgeous, village where the St. Lawrence met Lake Ontario took me over an hour. I headed away from the water for about three miles then turned onto a long, unplowed driveway that led to a farmhouse and barn a few hundred yards away. For what seemed like the hundredth time over the past month, I thanked the God of Technology for four-wheel drive and churned my way through the thick snow before coming to a stop in front of the house.

I was halfway out of the SUV when I heard barks and growls that raised the hairs on the back of my neck. I climbed back inside the vehicle and slammed the door shut just as an enormous Rottweiler hopped up on his back legs and snarled at me through the window. I tapped my horn to let Sofia Rossi know I was here, but the noise only annoyed the Rottweiler and his barks and snarls intensified as the nails on his front paws scratched at the glass.

"Nice to see you too," I said, impressed with the dog's intense focus.

Many breeds make excellent watchdogs. But the Rottweiler, at least the one daring me to step outside the vehicle, was a *guard* dog. And despite what I consider to be my excellent dog skills, there was no way I was opening the door until his owner had the beast well under control. An attractive, middle-aged woman with long black hair wearing a toque and parka stepped out onto the front porch and shook her head with a small smile as she walked down the shoveled path that led to where I was parked. She waved to me then rubbed the dog's head and pulled him off my car by the thick leather collar he was wearing. Only when she gestured that it was safe to get out did I slowly work my way from the car. I forced a smile at her while keeping a close eye on the Rottweiler that continued to stare at me with a low, guttural growl.

"Don't worry, he won't bite," she said.

"Does he know that?" I said, slowly lowering my bandaged hand in front of the dog's mouth.

She laughed and rubbed the Rottweiler's head.

"He's been trained to do that with strangers," she said.

"Well, he certainly paid attention in class."

"It cuts way down on the number of people popping in unannounced."

"Yeah, I'll bet," I said, standing still as the dog sniffed my hand. The Rottweiler must have liked the smell, and he nuzzled then licked my bandage. "What's his name?"

"Stinky."

"No wonder he's grumpy," I whispered.

"What?"

"Nothing. I'm just babbling," I said. "I'm Suzy Chandler."

"Sofia Rossi," she said, extending her hand. "Nice to meet you. Come on in. I've got a fresh pot of coffee, and I just made a batch of scones. Are you hungry?"

"I could eat."

I followed her up the steps into the house and looked around as I removed my coat. It was an old house but in great condition. Several paintings of dogs were hung on the walls, and it was furnished primarily with antiques. If she'd been going for early 1900's farmhouse, she'd nailed it.

"Have a seat," she said. "I'll be right back."

I sat down, and the Rottweiler dropped its head into my lap.

"You're a big baby, aren't you?" I said, scratching the dog's ears.

Then the dog decided he liked my leg. And he was about to prove just how much he liked it when Sofia came into the room carrying a tray.

"Stinky. Stop that. Get down," she said, shaking her head as she set the tray down. "I'm so sorry about that. He can be a little rambunctious from time to time."

"That's a word for it," I said. "I take it you've never had him fixed."

"No, he's used for breeding from time to time," she said, pouring two coffees. "He comes from a great lineage."

I added cream then took a sip and stared lovingly at the plate of scones.

"Try one," Sofia said. "And those are homemade strawberry preserves. I just can't resist the combination."

"Why even bother to try?" I said, laughing as I spread a generous portion of the preserves over one of the warm scones. I took a bite and nodded. "Fantastic."

"Thanks," she said, following my lead. "So, Mr. Provincial is looking for an Otterhound puppy?"

"He is," I said, taking another bite of my rapidly disappearing scone. "And you told him you were expecting a litter sometime in the spring?"

"I am," she said, drifting off for a moment. "At least, I'm still hopeful it will happen."

I slowly chewed the last bite as I tried to decide how to play the conversation. I settled on close to the vest and fell back on my tried and true guideline: When in doubt, ask a question.

"Is there a problem obtaining the litter?"

"I'm not sure," she said, for some reason tearing up. "The gentleman who owns the female Otterhound recently died."

"That's right," I said. "You mentioned over the phone that you had to go to a memorial service."

"I did."

"Skitch Friendly, right?"

"Yes, how did you know that?"

"Small town," I said, shrugging. "Have you spoken with the family to see if they're still interested in using your services?"

"No, I'm afraid I don't know the family. And I didn't get the chance to introduce myself yesterday," Sofia said. "All I know is that Skitch had a wife and two kids."

"Yes, he did," I said, reaching for another scone.

"Do you know them?" she said, holding her coffee with both hands as she sipped and glanced at me over the top of the mug.

"Yes, we've met a few times," I said.

"What are they like?"

"They're...an unusual family," I said.

"They'd have to be to live where they do," she said. "It's not a lifestyle I could handle."

"No argument there. When was the last time you saw Mr. Friendly?"

"It was probably a couple of months ago," she said, choosing her words carefully. "No, I take that back. I did see him briefly a few weeks ago. He stopped by to go over a few things about the Otterhound litter. Can I ask what you do for Mr. Provincial?"

"Paulie is my mom's boyfriend," I said, shrugging. "He's a friend and would have come himself, but he's on his way to Grand Cayman."

"Nice," she said, nodding.

"Can I ask you a question?"

"Sure," she said as she spread preserves onto her second scone.

"Otterhounds are incredibly rare. Do you contract with a breeder for the services of the male?"

"No," she said, sitting back in her chair. "I don't work with breeders. I've found most of them wanting to be what I would call...overly involved in the process."

"I see."

"You could say that my business approach is a bit unconventional."

"I assume that means that Paulie's puppy won't come with official papers," I said, studying her closely.

"No, I'm afraid that won't be possible," she said. "But you have my personal guarantee that the dog will be a one-hundred-percent purebred Otterhound."

"So, your clients are concerned about lineage?"

"Oh, they're very concerned with lineage," she said, nodding. "But most of them aren't worried about having the paperwork that goes along with it."

"Interesting."

"Most of my clients are only interested in acquiring a rare breed for themselves or their family," she said. "And I make it my personal mission to get it for them."

"Specialized work," I said, doing my best not to eat a third scone.

"Very."

"And expensive," I said. "Five grand is a lot of money for a dog."

"Actually, Mr. Provincial is fortunate that I'm able to find the Otterhounds locally. That's why he's only paying the five thousand. Many of my clients pay much more for their dogs."

"How on earth did you get started in this business?" I said, shaking my head.

"It is an odd way to make a living, isn't it?" she said, laughing. "A few years ago, I needed to get out of New York, and my father agreed to help set me up. Then he introduced me to a few people, and the business grew from there."

"What does your father do?"

Sofia laughed loud enough to get the Rottweiler's attention. Then she held out the plate of scones toward me, and I immediately caved and went in for a third. Besides, who knew how long this conversation was going to take, and if it kept snowing, I might end up stranded and starving on the side of the road.

"Suzy, if you're friends with Mr. Provincial, certainly you don't need to ask what my father does for a living."

"Yeah, good point," I said, taking a bite of my scone. "Do you have many dogs here?"

"No, just Stinky," she said, reaching down to pet the Rottweiler that was curled around her feet. "I just broker deals and sometimes supervise the insemination process. But I only do that when I'm worried about potential liability issues."

"Okay," I said, baffled. "Should I just tell Paulie that you'll be in touch with him as soon as you get some clarification about the Otterhound litter?"

"Yes, that's probably a good idea," Sofia said. "At some point, I'll need to figure out a way to get in touch with Mrs. Friendly."

"Good luck with that," I said, shaking my head. Then I caught the odd look she was giving me. "I mean, their place is way out in the woods. But I suppose I could give you directions."

"That would be helpful," she said. "Thank you."

"Well, it's the least I can do. I sort of have a vested interest in making sure Paulie gets his dog."

"Yes, I suppose you do," she said, setting her empty coffee mug down.

We both looked up when we heard the back door open then the sound of someone stamping snow off their feet.

"Man, it's really coming down out there," a man said from the kitchen.

My neurons flared as I tried to put a face to the familiar voice. But nothing registered.

"Okay, Ms. Rossi," the man said as he entered the room. "I've got what I need, so I'm going to head out while I still can get down the driveway. Next stop, Scranton. If everything goes to plan, I should be back no later than the weekend."

Then he stared at me with an open-mouthed expression that I returned.

"What are you doing here?" he said, blinking at me through his thick glasses.

"Great minds think alike," I said, staring at him. "I was just going to ask you the same question, Walter."

"I'm working," he said, removing his glasses and cleaning them with his sleeve. "What does it look like I'm doing?"

"I'm gonna go with wasting valuable oxygen."

"You two know each other?" Sofia said, glancing back and forth at us.

"Yeah, we've met a couple of times," I said. "What are you doing back here?"

"Like I just told you," he snapped. "I'm working."

"Walter occasionally does some odd jobs for me," Sofia said, deflecting.

"Well, if you're looking for odd, Walter's your guy," I said, still baffled to see Rooster's cousin standing in front of me.

"*You're* looking for a dog?" Walter said, laughing. "That's rich."

"I'm here for a friend," I said.

"Ms. Rossi," Walter said, pointing a finger at me. "Take my advice. Don't believe a word this woman tells you."

"I think I'm missing something," Sofia said, thoroughly confused.

"Walter and I have crossed swords a couple of times in the past," I said. "And his cousin Rooster had to have a little chat with him about the importance of playing nice with others."

Walter flinched at the mention of Rooster and began backing out of the room.

"I'll see you in a few days, Ms. Rossi," he said. "Remember what I told you. Don't believe a word that comes out of her mouth."

"Nice of him to drop in," I said after he'd departed. "What on earth does he do for you?"

"Basically, just some of the things I can't be bothered with," she said. "What did he do to you?"

"Tried to steal some dogs," I said.

"Really?" she said.

"Yeah, he's a wonderful human being," I said, getting up out of my chair. "And he's supposed to be in Florida."

"Walter tried to steal your dogs?" Sofia said. "As in plural?"

"He certainly did."

"How many dogs you do have?"

"As of this morning, sixty-eight," I said, pulling my coat on.

"Sixty-eight?"

"Yeah, but now that I know he's around, I'm going to go home and do another count."

# Chapter 14

Fortunately, the plows had been out while I was at Sofia Rossi's place, and the drive back to Clay Bay, while snowy, was uneventful. I called Rooster, got voicemail, and left a message for him to meet me at C's for lunch. Then I called Chief Abrams and left him the same message. My final call was to Josie who answered on the second ring.

"Hey," she said over the sound of barking dogs.

"What's going on over there? It sounds like there's a revolt in progress."

"Sammy's delivering the midday snack to all the dogs," she said, laughing. "And several of them apparently think he's taking too long. Did you meet with the Rossi woman?"

"I did," I said, pulling into the parking lot behind the restaurant. "Can you get away for lunch? I'm meeting Rooster and the Chief."

"The Chief?" Josie said. "Should I read anything into that?"

"Yeah, maybe," I said. "And I might need to pick your brain."

"Did you finally get all the way through what was left of yours?" she deadpanned.

"Funny. Can you make it?"

"Yeah, I can do that. I'll be there in fifteen. How are the roads?"

"They're a mess, so be careful," I said, getting out of the SUV and stepping down into six inches of fresh snow. "When are we going to Cayman?"

"Not soon enough. I'll see you in a few minutes."

I headed inside through the back door that led into the kitchen and saw Chef Claire sitting at the chef's table reading a book and sipping coffee. She bookmarked the page and set the book down.

"I didn't know you were coming in," she said.

"Slight change of plans," I said, removing my coat and hanging it up next to hers. "Slow day, huh?"

"Let's just say you won't have to wait long for your food," she said, getting to her feet. "Are you by yourself?"

"No, Josie's on her way. And so are Rooster and Chief Abrams if they get my message," I said as I scanned a menu.

"Is there a problem?" she said, raising an eyebrow at me.

"Maybe," I said. "Can you join us for lunch?"

"Yeah, I can make that work," Chef Claire said, then called out to Charlie who was standing in front of one of the stoves stirring a pot of soup. "I'm going to take a break and have lunch with Suzy. I assume you'll be able to handle things by yourself."

"Geez, I don't know, Chef Claire," Charlie said, glancing around the empty kitchen. "That's asking a lot."

"He thinks he's a comedian," Chef Claire said to me as we headed for the swinging doors that led into the dining room. "It's the door on the right."

"I knew that," I said, slowly pushing the door open. "Let's eat in front of the fire."

We headed for the lounge and found it empty except for Millie who was sitting on the customer side of the bar watching TV.

"Hey," she said, lowering the volume. "I can't believe it. Real human contact. What can I get you guys?"

"I'll stick with coffee," Chef Claire said.

"I'm good for now, Millie. Thanks."

Rooster and Josie entered through the front door and stomped snow off their feet before removing their coats. Rooster, as usual, was underdressed for the weather, and Josie was still wearing her scrubs. Chief Abrams arrived about a minute later, and he joined us in the lounge.

"Nice day, huh?" he said, glancing around.

"Yeah, if you live in the Arctic Circle," Josie said. "How's it going, Chief?"

"Better now that Suzy has offered to buy me lunch," he said. "What's good today, Chef Claire?"

"I'd go with the Reuben," she said. "And wash it down with a mug of the tomato bisque."

Everyone glanced at each other and nodded. Chef Claire called out to Millie.

"Millie, could you please buzz Charlie and let him know we'll need five orders of the soup and sandwich combo?" Chef Claire said.

"Okay, Suzy," Chief Abrams said. "I know you didn't get me down here just so you could feed me. What's up?"

"Something weird is going on," I said, frowning.

"Well, I figured that," the Chief said, glancing around with a big grin.

"Funny."

"But I'm going to need a bit more," the Chief said.

"I just came from a meeting with Sofia Rossi," I said.

"I have no idea who that is," the Chief said.

"She's the woman who was working with Skitch Friendly producing the Otterhound litters," I said.

"Okay," the Chief said. "But as they say in the old country, what does that have to do with the price of fish?"

"Her entire business seems to be acting as a broker for people looking to acquire rare dogs," I said.

"And you think she is somehow breaking the law?" Chief Abrams said.

"I'm not sure," I said, frowning. "She's very open about what she does, but since I was ostensibly there on Paulie's behalf, maybe she thought she didn't need to be secretive about it."

"She's somehow connected to organized crime?" the Chief said.

"I'm sure of it," I said. "In fact, she openly admitted it."

"Rossi?" the Chief said, frowning. "The name doesn't ring a bell."

"Her maiden name is Carlucci," I said.

"Her father is Mikey the Mechanic?" the Chief said, surprised.

"Yeah, Michael Carlucci," I said. "You know who he is?"

"Sure. He's a heavy hitter in the City. At least, he used to be. I think he's pretty much retired these days. What the heck is his daughter doing around here?"

"She said she needed to get out of New York, and her father set her up in the dog business."

"Okay. But I'm still not following where you're going with this," the Chief said.

"Me either," Josie said as she tossed another log on the fire.

"I could be wrong, but I think she was working with Friendly just to help him out a bit financially. It was like she had a soft spot for him."

"A soft spot for Skitch?" Rooster said. "That's a stretch."

"When I mentioned that the five thousand she quoted for an Otterhound puppy was a lot of money, she waved it off like it was nothing. I got the feeling she did those litters as a favor to him." I looked at Josie. "What are some of the numbers you've heard that rare dogs can go for?"

"Well, lately, the Tibetan Mastiffs have become a major status symbol. Especially for rich Chinese. If I wanted to get into the rare dog business, that would be the breed I'd be looking at. I read about one going for a million and a half about a year ago."

"A million-five?" the Chief said. "For a dog?"

"For a very rare dog," Josie said. "That's obviously an outlier, but it wouldn't surprise me to hear about Mastiff puppies going for a hundred thousand."

"Man, I'm in the wrong business," the Chief said. "So, she's a high-end breeder?"

"No, she made it perfectly clear that she doesn't like to work with breeders," I said. "She said they tend to stick their nose where it doesn't belong."

"Then she's definitely working the black market," Josie said. "With no breeder involvement, you'd have a lot of problems getting the dog's lineage records."

"A dog's lineage is important to a lot of people, right?" the Chief said.

"It's vital," Josie said. "At least, if you're breeding purebred dogs or have any plans to show them. If you just want a cool dog, it's not a necessity."

"She said she guarantees that all her dogs are one hundred percent purebred," I said.

"Well, if I was paying that much, I would certainly hope so," the Chief said, shaking his head.

"Did she have a lot of dogs at her place?" Josie said.

"No, just one. A Rottweiler named Stinky."

"That's cruel," Josie said, laughing. "The poor dog."

"This is all very interesting, Suzy," Rooster said. "But what does it have to do with me? Not that I'm complaining about the free lunch."

"That's the *really* interesting part of the story," I said, giving him a small smile. "I met someone who works for her, and you'll never guess who it is."

"For the sake of saving time, let's assume you're right," Rooster said. "Who was it?"

"Your cousin. Walter."

"What?" Rooster said, his voice rising.

"Coke Bottle?" Josie said.

"That moron who stole Al and Dente?" Chef Claire said.

"And don't forget the Dandie Dinmont," Josie said.

"That's the one," I said, turning to Rooster. "I thought you banished him to Florida."

"I thought I did too," Rooster said. "What the heck is he doing working for her?"

"They didn't say," I said, shrugging. "But I do have a working theory."

"Here we go," Josie said, laughing. "This is always my favorite part."

"Shut it," I said, making a face at her. "Since Sofia doesn't work with breeders, that means she somehow needs to find available females capable of producing litters."

"Nothing gets past you," Josie said, still laughing.

"But she doesn't actually keep the dogs on site," I said. "So, we can assume that she is paying those people to take good care of their dog and the puppies until they're ready to go."

"And those people wouldn't have to deal with the problem of trying to sell all the puppies individually," Josie said, nodding. "Yeah, I can see where that might appeal to some folks."

"Especially if Sofia is paying them big bucks," I said.

"But what about the other half of the transaction?" Chef Claire said. "She still needs to find a male to breed them with."

"That's where Rooster's cousin comes in," I said, tossing my line into the water to see what sort of reaction I got.

"Coke Bottle is stealing the males?" Chef Claire said, frowning. "He should have learned his lesson by now. If he's stealing rare dogs, their owners would be reporting it to the cops immediately."

"No, he's not actually stealing the dogs," I said, glancing around with a grimace. "Just a part of the dog."

I waited out a long silence as they pondered my comment.

"Oh, no," Josie said, scowling. "That's disgusting."

"My cousin is a dog semen thief?" Rooster said.

"Well, this is a lovely conversation to have over lunch," Chef Claire said.

"Think about it," I said. "It would be easy enough to find out where some of the top-end, rare-breed dogs live. Especially if the owner shows the dog or advertises stud services."

"And then Coke Bottle does what?" Chef Claire said. "Sneak into where the dog lives and collect samples?"

"Yeah."

"We really should have had you checked for a concussion when you got hit by the door," Chef Claire said. "That's nuts."

"No, just think about it," I said, glancing over at her.

"Suzy, I'm doing everything I can not to think about it," Chef Claire said. "Yuk."

"I'm sure breeders do it all the time," I said.

"Good for the breeders," Chef Claire said.

"Well, given what we know about Coke Bottle's social life, I'm sure he's immensely qualified for the job," Josie deadpanned.

Everyone, including me, laughed long and hard.

Millie approached carrying a large tray.

"You sure you guys don't want to sit at a table?" she said.

"No, this is good," Josie said. "And the fire feels great."

"Okay, just try not to spill it all over yourself," Millie said, shrugging as she passed out our soup and sandwiches.

"Hey, I haven't spilled in at least a week," Josie said, reaching for her sandwich.

I took a sip of the bisque from my mug and nodded at Chef Claire.

"Good?" she said, taking a sip.

"A total knee-buckler," I said, then gave my Reuben a loving stare. "I think I might have an idea why nobody knew that the Otterhound was pregnant."

"Was Sofia still talking about a spring litter?" Josie said through a mouthful of corned beef as a trail of Thousand Island dressing dribbled down her chin.

"You're leaking," I said, tossing her a napkin. "She specifically mentioned the spring. Which means she's completely out of the loop about Gabby's condition."

"So, what's your theory?" the Chief said.

"I'm wondering if Coke Bottle got his hands on some Otterhound semen and decided to inseminate the dog," I said, refocusing on my bisque and turning toward Rooster. "Your cousin ended up hiding in your cabin out in the woods both times we dealt with him."

"He did," Rooster said, nodding. "Chef Claire, how do you this? It's just soup and a sandwich."

"Thanks, Rooster," she said, beaming at him. "You're so sweet."

"And your property bumps up against the Friendly's at some point, right?"

"Yes, it certainly does."

"Would your cousin know that? I mean, would he be familiar with the Friendly's property?"

"Sure, that's definitely a possibility," Rooster said. "Walter loves to hike in the woods. At least, he used to. You think he inseminated the dog and has plans to steal her at some point?"

"I can't think of any other explanation," I said. "Nobody at the house and probably not even Skitch knew that the dog was pregnant."

"Maybe Skitch figured out what was going on and confronted Coke Bottle about it?" Chef Claire said.

"And then Coke Bottle shot him?" Josie said, frowning.

"Not with his eyesight," Rooster said. "He can't see a foot in front of him."

"How about with a powerful scope?" Chef Claire said.

"Maybe," Rooster said, frowning. "But it's highly unlikely."

"He did only hit him in the shoulder," Josie said. "Maybe he was aiming for something else."

"Walter is a hunter," Rooster said, shrugging. "But he's just not a very good one."

"No, I don't like it," the Chief said. "If Friendly's death wasn't accidental, I still like acquiring the gas lease rights as the motive."

"Yeah, me too," I said. "But something about this dog operation is bothering me. It has to be connected in some way."

"I don't see how," the Chief said. "I think we've just got two parallel situations playing out. So, what now, Snoopmeister?"

"Well, I'd like to take a look around when we go back to the Friendly's place," I said.

"Why are you going back there?" Chef Claire said.

"We're going to buy it," I said.

"You're going to buy hundreds of acres of land in the middle of the woods?" Chef Claire said.

"Well, my mother and Rooster and I are," I said.

"She does keep us on our toes, doesn't she?" Chef Claire said to Josie.

"She certainly does," Josie said, laughing. "Let me guess, you're going to buy it just so 3E can't get its hands on the lease rights?"

"That's the plan," Rooster said, draining the last of his bisque.

"Won't that upset Mr. Billows?" Josie said.

"We can only hope," I said. "If he's somehow involved in Friendly's death, then he must be desperate to acquire the lease rights. Us buying it just might get him to tip his hand and do something stupid." I noticed Chef Claire and Josie staring at me. "What? Did I spill?"

"I'm just sitting here thinking about what a uniquely weird person you are," Josie said.

Chef Claire snorted.

"You got something to add?" I said, glaring at her.

"Great minds think alike?" she said, laughing.

"Okay, Snoopmeister, knock yourself out," Josie said. "But that really doesn't get you any closer to what's going on with the dog operation."

"No, it doesn't," I said, glancing over at Rooster. "But Coke Bottle did mention that he was heading to Scranton. Does that mean anything to you? Do you have any family in that neck of the woods?"

"Nope," Rooster said.

I sat quietly for the next few minutes munching on my sandwich. My neurons were working overtime, but nothing coalesced.

"Well, how about that?" Josie said, staring down at her phone.

"What is it?"

"Take a look," she said, handing me the phone.

"Wow," I said, shaking my head.

"What is it?" Chef Claire said, leaning forward to read from the screen. "Purebred Tibetan Mastiffs. The breeder is located right outside of Scranton."

"Yes," I said, scrolling. "And the breeder's male is the top-rated Mastiff in the country."

"I take it all back," Chef Claire said. "When I grow up, I want to be just like you."

"An annoying overeater with no fashion sense?" Josie deadpanned.

I tried to scowl at her but ended up laughing.

"Okay, I gotta give you that one," I said. "That was good."

"You think Coke Bottle is headed there?" Chef Claire said.

"I can't think of any other reason he'd be going to Scranton," Rooster said. "Do I see a road trip in our future?"

"You'd be willing to go with me?" I said.

"Absolutely," Rooster said. "I need to have a little chat with my cousin."

"If the weather clears a bit, we could go tomorrow."

"No, tomorrow is no good," Rooster said. "We need to pay a visit to Jessie Friendly before she decides to sell those lease rights. I already talked to your mom, and we're heading out there first thing in the morning."

"But that walk from the car to their house is going be brutal in all this snow," I said, shaking my head.

"Yes, it would," Rooster said. "That's why we're going to ski in."

"We're going to go cross-country skiing in the morning?"

"We are."

"Crap."

# Chapter 15

I sat down in the Otterhound's condo and gently placed Gabby's head in my lap. I rubbed her ears while Josie examined the bandage on the dog's front leg.

"That's good for at least another day," she said, sitting down next to the dog and inserting her stethoscope into her ears. "See if you can get her to roll over onto her back."

I began scratching the Otterhound's side, and soon she rolled over in my lap. I worked on her extended belly for a few moments then moved my hand to give Josie room. She listened closely as she moved the stethoscope around the dog's stomach.

"I think I'm picking up six heartbeats today," she said, sliding the instrument into her lab coat. "Maybe the little guy is moving around."

"That's great," I said, hugging the Otterhound. "She has to be close to delivering, right?"

"She has to be," Josie said, removing a bag of bite-sized from her coat and holding it out.

I grabbed a small handful and opened one with my good hand.

"No, these aren't for you," I said to the Otterhound who was paying close attention to what was in my hand. I reached into my pocket and removed a plastic bag of Chef Claire's dog jerky and gave her a piece. "This is your snack."

"If she doesn't deliver soon, we'll need to get her moving around," Josie said. "I hate to do it given that leg."

"She doesn't seem to be in pain."

"Yeah, I know, but she's not moving around on it much," Josie said, climbing to her feet. "I'm gonna give her a few more days and trust that she'll know when it's time. When are you leaving today?"

"Rooster and my mom are going to swing by to pick me up," I said. "They said around nine."

"Is that what you're wearing?"

I glanced down at the thick pair of sweatpants I had on over thermal underwear along with two flannel shirts and a bulky sweater.

"Yeah. What's wrong with it?"

"Nothing," she said, shaking her head with a small smile. "You always rock Vintage Lumberjack. It looks good on you."

"Shut it."

"You're going to sweat like crazy in that outfit. Why don't you just borrow the one-piece you got Chef Claire for Christmas?"

"No way," I said. "You've seen how tight that thing is."

"So?"

"It's too…revealing."

"Suzy, you'd be covered from head to toe," she said, frowning.

"You know what I mean."

"Okay, have it your way. But don't forget your chainsaw."

"Funny," I said, gently punching her on the shoulder. "It's going to be freezing out there."

"Maybe Cooter will make you a matching squirrel sweater," Josie said.

"That's just what I need," I said, climbing to my feet.

"And don't forget to wear the hat," she said.

"What?"

"Hey, you're trying to convince his family to sell you their property," Josie said. "You don't want to do anything that might hurt Cooter's feelings and ruin your chances to close the deal."

"Now you're just screwing with me, right?

"Maybe," she deadpanned.

Sammy poked his head through the door.

"Your mom and Rooster are here," he said, then disappeared back into the registration area.

We said our goodbyes to the Otterhound and left the condo area. On the way to registration, just to be on the safe side, I grabbed the squirrel hat from a closet I'd tossed it in the day Cooter gave it to me. I stuffed it into the pocket of my sweatpants as I entered the registration area and shook my head when I got a look at my mother's outfit. She was wearing an identical outfit to the one I'd given Chef Claire, but hers was hot pink.

"At least you won't have to worry about being mistaken for a deer," I said, grinning.

"It's nice to see you too, darling. Is that what you're wearing?"

"Yes."

"Where did I go wrong, Rooster?" my mother said with a sigh. "Okay, Paul Bunyan, you win. Are you ready to go?"

"I am," I said. "I just need to grab my skis. They're right outside the back door."

"I'll grab them," Rooster said, heading for the condo area. "I'll meet you outside."

I waved goodbye to Josie and Jill and followed my mother down the front steps to Rooster's truck.

"How much do you think Mrs. Friendly is going to want for the property?" I said, grabbing a handful of snow off the roof of the truck and making a snowball.

"Now that she knows there's a reservoir of natural gas under the ground, probably a lot," my mother said, keeping a close eye on the snowball in my hand. "Don't you dare."

"The thought never crossed my mind," I said, grinning at her. Then something popped into my head that I'd been wondering about for a while. "Hey, Mom. Whatever happened to your plans to develop the property you own behind the Inn? Your last idea was to turn it into a zoo."

"I took a look at it," she said. "But it would have been a nightmare dealing with all the issues that popped up right from the start. And at my age, who needs a hassle like that?"

"So, you're just going to leave it undeveloped?"

"Actually, darling, I have been thinking about what to do with it," she said.

"And?"

"I thought I'd give it to you and Josie," she said, taking a step back to give Rooster room to attach my skis to the roof.

"What on earth would we do with it?" I said, staring out at the woods that ran behind our fenced play area.

"Expand," she said with a big grin. "I'm thinking about a multi-county rescue program."

"What?" I said.

"You do such wonderful work," she said, shrugging. "It seems like a shame not to expand it. In addition to dogs, you could also take care of horses and a host of other animals."

"Mom, we'd need to hire a couple more full-time vets and at least another dozen staff to handle something that size."

"So?" she said, giving me a blank stare.

I studied her face closely. She was giving me her best *I really don't see what the problem is* look, so I merely nodded.

"Let me run it by Josie," I said eventually.

"That's my girl," she said as she opened the door and gestured for me to climb into the back seat.

Rooster hopped in and started the truck. He glanced over at my mother then at me through the rearview mirror.

"Are we all set?" he said, putting the truck into gear.

"I believe we are," my mother said.

"Did you bring your hat?" Rooster said with a grin.

"Yeah, I've got it," I said. "Josie said I had to bring it along just in case Cooter asks about it."

"You got a new hat?" my mother said, glancing back at me.

"Yup."

"Well, let me see it," my mother said, half-turning in her seat.

"No, that's okay, Mom," I said, shaking my head.

"Don't be silly," she said. "Let me see your hat."

I pulled the hat from my pocket, punched it back into some semblance of shape and placed it on my head. It covered my forehead and was only kept from going further down my face by the tops of my ears. I cocked my head and struck a pose.

"Wow," she said, dumbfounded.

"Nice, huh?"

"Well, at least it goes with the rest of your outfit."

"Funny," I said, pushing the hat up off my forehead.

"Tragic," she said, unable to take her eyes off the hat. "Simply tragic."

# Chapter 16

"Darling, I've found that it's much easier when both skis are actually pointing in the same direction."

"Yeah, thanks for the tip, Mom," I said, lifting one foot to reposition the recalcitrant ski.

We'd been making the trek from Rooster's truck to the Friendly's cabin for about twenty minutes through close to a foot of fresh snow. I was sweating profusely and cursing under my breath. At least, I thought it was under my breath.

"Watch the language, darling," my mother said over her shoulder as she continued to expertly work her way through the snow.

"Are we there yet?" I said as a trickle of cold sweat ran down the middle of my back.

"You need a break?" Rooster said over his shoulder without breaking stride.

"I need a doctor."

"Hang in there," Rooster said, laughing. "Only a couple more hours to go."

"You're really not funny, Rooster," I said, digging my poles into the snow and churning forward.

We came to a sudden stop when we heard the first gunshot. Then we heard several more in rapid succession.

"It's okay," Rooster said. "It's not hunters. Cooter is probably doing some target shooting."

We resumed our trek and ten minutes later came to the fence that bordered the Friendly's cabin. I removed my skis, stuck them upright in the snow, then knelt down to massage my burning calves. The gunshots continued, and it sounded like they were coming from the far side of the cabin. We were about a hundred feet from the porch when the front door opened and Very stepped outside waving.

"What a nice surprise," she called out. "But you must be freezing. Come on in."

I climbed the short set of steps breathing heavily and gave her a quick hug.

"How are you doing, Very?"

"I'm good," she said, beaming. "Hi, Rooster." Then she looked at my mother. "You're Suzy's mom, aren't you?"

"I am," my mother said, extending her hand. "It's been a long time, Very."

"I love your outfit," Very said, nodding. "Pink's my favorite color."

"Thank you."

"Let's go inside," Very said, holding the door open for us.

We walked inside, and I was impressed with the way the cabin had been designed and decorated. Skitch Friendly may have been a recluse, but he obviously knew his way around a set of tools. The open space we were standing in dominated the cabin, and it was warm and toasty. I removed my coat and realized my sweater was soaked with sweat. Outside, the sound of gunfire continued.

"Have a seat," Very said, heading for the kitchen area. "We have coffee and tea. Or if you like, I'll pour you some of Mama's shine."

"Maybe just a smidgen," Rooster said, holding his thumb and forefinger about an inch apart.

"I suppose I could have one," my mother said, nodding. "Thanks."

"You got it," Very said. "How about you, Suzy?"

I frowned as I remembered my previous encounter with Jessie Friendly's deadly concoction and shook my head.

"Coffee's fine, thanks," I said. "Let me give you a hand."

I followed her into the kitchen and watched as Very carefully poured two healthy portions of the clear liquid then grabbed an old-time coffee pot from the top of the wood stove and filled a mug.

"So, how was the rest of your date?" I said.

"It was great getting out of the house," Very said. "And he's nice enough, I guess." Then she shrugged. "I just think I can do better."

"Good for you," I said, following her back to where my mother and Rooster were sitting.

Very passed the drinks around, set a tray of fresh biscuits and honey on the table in front of us, then sat down across from us.

"Help yourself," she said. "I just made them."

We each grabbed one of the warm biscuits and slathered honey. We ate in silence as Very continued to glance back and forth at us.

"So, what brings you out here?" she said after we'd devoured our first biscuit.

"We'd like to talk to your mom," Rooster said.

"She's out back with Cooter," Very said, getting to her feet. "He just got a new scope for his rifle that he's having trouble getting sighted." She walked toward a door on the far side of the cabin then paused and looked back at us. "Multiple visitors on the same day. That's a first."

"You're expecting someone else?" Rooster said.

"Yes," Very said, grinning. "Herman is supposed to drop by later."

She headed out the door, and my mother continued to stare at her through the window as Very headed down a flight of stairs.

"She seems remarkably well adjusted," my mother said. "And very bright."

"She is," I said, nodding.

"So, Mr. Billows is on his way," Rooster said. "Looks like we got here just in time."

"Are you really sure we need to buy this place?" I said.

They both nodded.

"But there's a chance that fracking is never going to be allowed again," I said.

"You want to explain it?" Rooster said to my mother.

"No, you go ahead," she said, reaching for a second biscuit.

"Your mother and I could never live with ourselves if we didn't do everything we could to stop it," he said, then took a sip of shine. "Man, this is really good."

"I'll take your word for it," I said.

"And if fracking was ever made legal down the road after we're gone, everyone would know who dropped the ball."

"You're worried about your legacy?" I said, frowning.

"No, darling," my mother said. "We're worried about a bunch of poison getting into the groundwater and ending up in the River. But, yes, I would much rather be remembered as someone who helped prevent it from happening as opposed to being labeled an enabler."

"Fair enough," I said, shrugging. "But I'm not sure why I need to be part of the deal."

"Because one day it's all going to be yours," she said. "And you might as well be involved right from the start."

The door opened, and Jessie Friendly entered. She slipped her snowy boots off and closed the door behind her then walked across the room with a confused look on her face.

"Hi, Jessie," Rooster said, standing up.

"No, sit," she said, waving him back onto the couch. "Very said you wanted to talk to me."

"We do," Rooster said.

"Okay," she said, sitting down in the chair Very had just vacated. "If you were willing to make that trek all the way in, the least I can do is listen to what you have to say."

"Very mentioned that Herman Billows is stopping by later," Rooster said.

"So, that's what this is all about?" she said, frowning as she glanced back and forth at us. "Now that you've found something buried on my property you want, I guess I'll never be lonely, huh?"

"No, it's not like that, Jessie," Rooster said, shaking his head.

"He's offering me a lot of money for those lease rights," she said. "And a whole lot more if the government ever changes its mind and lets them start drilling."

"Has Very been talking with you about moving?" I said. "To someplace warmer?"

"That's all we've been talking about. And we're thinking seriously about doing it," Jessie said. "I'm not sure how I'll handle being back in civilization, but I'm sure looking forward to giving it a shot."

"What about Cooter?" Rooster said.

"Cooter will never leave this place," Jessie said, shaking her head. Then she grinned. "I'm sure gonna miss that boy."

We all laughed along with her, then she turned serious again.

"So, why are you here? You thinking about maybe beating Mr. Willows' offer?"

"Actually, Jessie," Rooster said. "We're thinking about buying your property."

"Buying it?" she said, frowning. "Why would you want to do that?"

"So we can keep people like Mr. Billows from ever getting their hands on it," my mother said.

"You really think this fracking stuff is that bad?" Jessie said.

"Let's just say that we aren't willing to take that chance," she said. "If it comes down to a choice between a well-lit room or clean drinking water, I'll sit in the dark any day."

"What would you do with the place?" Jessie said.

"Not a thing," my mother said. "In fact, Cooter would be welcome to live here for as long as he wants."

"But he'd have to pay you rent, right?"

"No," my mother said, shaking her head. "He can continue to live here for free."

"How much of my shine have you people been drinking?" she said, obviously concerned that we were up to something nefarious.

"If you're willing to sell us your property, Jessie, we would own virtually all of the acreage where they've found that gas reserve."

"And you'd just sit on the land?"

"Yes, we would," Rooster said. "Eventually, all of it will pass to Suzy. And she's made the same commitment to leave it untouched."

"I probably shouldn't tell you this," Jessie said. "But I don't have a clue what it's worth."

"We don't either, Jessie," my mother said. "But we have a general idea. What we're proposing is that we get a couple of appraisers out here to take a look. Based on what they come up with, I'm sure we'll be able to give you more than a fair price for it."

"And you'd be willing to put the part about Cooter being able to live here in the contract?" she said, staring at my mother.

"You can put anything you want in the contract," my mother said, shrugging. "Except for allowing any deep drilling."

"Mr. Billows is coming out here with a contract today," Jessie said. "What do I tell him?"

"Tell him no," Rooster said. "Or better yet, tell him you're selling the property, and the new owners aren't interested in leasing the land."

"He's not going to like that," Jessie said.

"I'm sure he'll get over it," Rooster said.

"Things sure have changed in a week," Jessie said, staring out the window. "First, Skitch. Now, this." Then she focused on my mother. "So, how would this work?"

My mother reached into her backpack and pulled out an envelope. She handed it to Jessie who opened it and removed a single sheet of paper.

"That's a letter indicating your intent to sell us your property. It's good for thirty days, and if we aren't able to come to an agreement by then, it becomes invalid. Over the next few days, we'll get the appraisals done then make you an offer. And as soon as we agree on a price, we'll write you a check."

"Just like that?" Jessie said, perusing the letter.

"Just like that," Rooster said.

My mother again reached into her backpack and removed her checkbook. She wrote the check, signed it, then handed it to Jessie.

"And just so you're convinced that we're serious, we'd like to give this to you as a down payment."

Jessie stared at the check, then stared at my mother.

"This is just the down payment?" she said.

"It is," my mother said. "And I'm sure the next check we give you will be much bigger."

Jessie stared down at the check again and blinked several times.

"What do you think?" Rooster said.

"I think it's time for Very and I to start looking at condos."

The door opened, and Very and Cooter entered after stomping snow off their boots. Cooter was holding a large piece of paper with a bullseye, and he beamed when he spotted me.

"Hi, Suzy," he said. "Where's your hat?"

"It's right here, Cooter," I said, removing it from my pocket and waving it in the air. "I always take my hat off inside."

"So, you like it?"

"Love it," I said.

"That's great," Cooter said, then focused on his mother. "Mama, that sight still ain't working right. Take a look."

He held up the target and pointed at it.

"My first shot is always dead on, then they start drifting up and to the left. See?"

"Cooter, how many times do I have to tell you that you need to tap the turret a few times after you've made your sight adjustments? That will lock in the changes you've made. Your first shot is obviously bumping them back to where they were."

"Oh, yeah," he said, frowning. "I forgot." He looked around, flashed me a smile, then headed for the door. "It was nice seeing you, Suzy."

Jessie watched her son head back outside with a slow shake of her head.

"I sure hope he'll be okay out here all by himself," she said.

"He'll be fine," Very said. "He loves being alone. What did I miss?"

"Have a seat," Jessie said. "I have some news for you."

"Actually, I think we'll get going, Jessie," Rooster said. "It's coming down hard, and I'd like to get on the road."

"Okay," Jessie said, handing Very the check. "So, I'll hear from you soon?"

"You certainly will," my mother said, getting to her feet and extending her hand. "Thank you, Jessie. You've done a wonderful thing."

"What's going on?" Very said, staring at her mother.

"I'll tell you in a minute," she said, escorting us to the front door. "Drive safe."

We were all the way across the front lawn when I heard Very's excited screams coming from inside the cabin.

"I think she likes the idea," my mother said, laughing as she knelt down to put her skis on.

I groaned as I did the same and was soon poling my way across the snow in the direction of Rooster's truck. Another couple of inches had fallen since we'd arrived, and I was already totally sick and tired of winter even though it had only officially begun about a week ago.

"Are you and Paulie still flying out tomorrow?" I said, then groaned as my back protested.

"We are," she said, glancing back over her shoulder. "It was eighty-two in Grand Cayman this morning."

"Good for Grand Cayman."

"When do you think the Otterhound is going to deliver?"

"It has to be soon," I said, then my neurons flared briefly. "Hey, hang on a sec."

"What?" my mother said, picking up the pace.

"Jessie never mentioned the dog once the whole time we were there," I said, frowning.

"You're right," Rooster said. "She didn't."

"That must mean she's only interested in the money she'll get for the puppies," I said. "She doesn't give a crap about Gabby."

"Darling, don't jump to any conclusions," my mother said. "The woman just lost her husband, and now she's about to sell her property. I'm sure it just slipped her mind."

"Yeah, maybe," I said, still grumpy about it. "But still."

"Just try to focus on your skiing," my mother said.

"Actually, I'm doing everything I can not to think about it, Mom. My back and legs are on fire. And I'm freezing my butt off."

"Put your hat on," Rooster said. "That oughta help."

"Shut it," I said, then frowned and came to a stop when I saw a man trudging toward us. "Well, look who's here."

Rooster and my mother also stopped, and we watched Herman Billows do his best to work his way through the thick blanket of snow. He had his head down but finally spotted us and greeted us with a small wave.

"Hey," Billows said, coming to a stop right in front of us. "I can't believe you're out here by choice."

"We had a meeting," my mother said.

"With Jessie Friendly?" Billows said, surprised. He brushed snow off his head and shoulders and looked as miserable as I felt.

"As a matter of fact, yes," Rooster said.

"Can I ask you why?"

"We just bought her property," my mother said.

Herman Billows flinched, then glared at us.

"You're joking, right?"

"I'd never joke about something like that," my mother said.

"But I already have a tentative verbal agreement with her," Billows said, hunkered down against the wind.

"A *tentative verbal*?" my mother said, laughing. "I'm no expert, Mr. Billows, but I'm willing to bet my lawyer would have a field day with that argument."

"You've made a big mistake," Billows said. "I do not like to be screwed with."

"Nobody is screwing with you, Mr. Billows," my mother said. "The Friendly's property is adjacent to ours, and we thought it would fit perfectly into our plans."

"Plans to do what?"

"Absolutely nothing," Rooster said. "That's our plan."

"And I'm afraid that lease rights aren't included as part of our do-nothing plan," my mother said.

"Well, I guess we'll just see about that," Billows said, storming off.

"He's really not dressed right for this weather," my mother said, staring after him.

"No, he's not," Rooster said. "He's probably going to catch one heck of a cold."

"Or a serious case of frostbite," I said.

"That would work," my mother said, nodding before she continued her trek back to the truck. "C'mon, let's go. Who's up for lunch at C's?"

"Rhetorical, right?" Rooster said to me.

"Nothing gets past you."

## Chapter 17

Early the next morning, I picked Rooster up then drove south on Route 81. The trip to Scranton, weather permitting, should take less than four hours, and, so far, the sun was out, and the roads were clear. I put the cruise control on seventy and wiggled my toes. Yesterday's cross-country adventure had left my back and legs aching, and I was pretty much a physical mess. But the bruise on my nose was healing, I'd be getting my stitches out in a couple of days, and if I could manage to get rid of the cramps in my legs, I'd almost be back to full strength.

"Where would you rank this trip on the list of crazy ideas?" I said, glancing over at Rooster in the passenger seat.

"Your list or mine?" he said, grinning. "If we're talking about you, this doesn't crack the top hundred."

"So, I'm not nuts," I said, laughing. "Remember to tell that to my mother."

"I think it's a great idea," Rooster said, moving his seat back and reclining.

"What are you going to do to your cousin when we find him?"

"You'll see," he said. "At least some of it."

We crossed the New York-Pennsylvania border and continued our southern journey until we started seeing the

Scranton exits. I left the interstate and headed west for about ten miles then spotted the sign for Highland Hills Breeders. I made a right and drove up a short driveway and parked. We climbed out of the SUV and took a look around. Then I heard an impressive, deep bark coming from inside a fenced area next to the house.

"Wow," I said, trying to catch a glimpse of the dog. "That's quite a bark."

"It certainly is," Rooster said. "And he's not shy about using it."

We took a few steps to our left and got our first look at the dog.

"Look at the size of him," I said, staring in awe at the Mastiff. "I thought Captain was big."

"Do you take him for a walk or just ride him?" Rooster said, laughing. "My goodness. He's gorgeous."

"Magnificent," I said, taking a few steps closer then stopped when the dog started barking louder.

The front door opened, and a man waved at us. Rooster and I headed for the porch, and he met us at the bottom of the steps.

"Hi, how are you doing?" he said, sizing both of us up.

"Hello. Are you Mr. Highland?" I said.

"I am," he said. "Please call me Roger."

"I'm Suzy. And this is Rooster."

"Nice to meet you," he said. "What can I do for you folks?"

"We'd like to talk to you about one of your dogs," I said.

"I'm afraid we aren't expecting a new litter until sometime in the summer."

"No, we aren't looking for a puppy," I said, pointing at the fenced area where the Mastiff was keeping a close eye on us. "We'd like to talk about him."

"Chi?" he said, frowning. "What about him?"

"He's the top stud Mastiff in the country, right?" I said.

"He certainly is," he said with pride. "You want to say hi to him?"

"Absolutely," I said.

"Just make sure you give him a few minutes to get used to you," Roger said. "He can be a little protective."

We followed him to the fenced area and stood back as he opened the gate. The Mastiff accepted a quick pet from Roger, then lumbered over to us. The dog smelled both of us as he circled then nudged the side of my leg. I stumbled, and Rooster reached out and grabbed my arm to keep me from falling.

"That's his love tap," Roger said, laughing. "He likes you."

"He's beautiful," I said, running my hands through the Mastiff's thick red fur.

"Yeah, he's pretty special."

"And unique, right?" Rooster said.

"Around here, he certainly is. I imagine there's some like him in Asia," Roger said. "So, why are you here? Do you have a female you'd like to breed with him?"

"No," I said, kneeling down to hug the dog. "Oh, I love this guy. We're here because we think there might be a man in the area with plans to steal some of Chi's semen." I frowned when I heard the words come out of my mouth. "That probably sounds very strange."

"It's definitely not what I expected to hear," Roger said. "What makes you think that?"

"We've stumbled onto a black-market operation that deals in rare dogs," I said.

"I've heard about them," he said, nodding. "But they've never come near me before."

"These dogs go for a fortune in China," I said.

"Tell me about it," he said, pointing at his house. "How do you think I was able to afford this place?"

"So, you sell puppies in China?" I said.

"Only one," he said. "But it was a major pain in the neck dealing with the bureaucracy. And there are enough people in the States looking for these guys. It's not nearly as much money, but we're doing just fine." He lovingly thumped the dog's side. "Aren't we, Chi?"

The dog barked loudly and nudged Roger's leg.

"Do you bring him inside at night?" Rooster said.

"Of course," Roger said. "He's got his own room right off the kitchen where he likes to sleep."

"Have you had anybody stop by recently asking about puppies?"

"As a matter of fact, a guy stopped by yesterday," Roger said, surprised. "A weird looking guy."

"Is this him?" Rooster said, handing him a photograph.

"That's him," Roger said, nodding. "I'll never forget those glasses. They must be an inch thick." He handed the photo back. "Are you guys cops?"

"No," I said, shaking my head. "We're just trying to figure out what is going on with a pregnant Otterhound back at home."

"Otterhound? They're pretty rare, too," Roger said. "Where's home?"

"A place called Clay Bay in the Thousand Islands," Rooster said.

"Sure, I've been fishing up there," he said. "Beautiful spot."

"Yes, it is," Rooster said.

"You think this guy might be coming back?" Roger said.

"We do," I said. "He didn't give you a phone number or happen to mention where he was staying, did he?"

"No," Roger said, shaking his head. "As soon as I told him I wouldn't have any dogs until the summer he headed off."

"What was he driving?" Rooster said.

"It was an older truck. Dark blue with New York plates."

"Are there any motels close to here?" I said.

"Yeah, there's a couple places just up the road," he said, pointing. "But they're both pretty crappy."

"Thanks, Roger," I said, again kneeling down to hug the Mastiff. "You take good care of this guy."

"You think I should let the cops know this guy's around?"

"No, that won't be necessary," Rooster said. "We've got this. But keep a close eye on this guy for a few days."

"I always do," Roger said, then shook his head. "People sure do come up with some strange ways to make money." He reached into his pocket and removed a business card. "I'd appreciate it if you'd give me a call and let me know what you find out."

"We'll do that," Rooster said, sliding the card into his pocket. "Thanks for all your help."

"No problem," Roger said. "Should I put you on the list for a puppy?"

"No, but thanks for offering," Rooster said, catching sight of the look in my eyes and jumping in before I could respond. "We're all set with dogs."

"There's always room for one more," I said, again rubbing the dog's head.

"No," Rooster said. "Let's go."

We waved goodbye and climbed back into the SUV. Rooster glanced over at me and shook his head.

"You were going to say yes, weren't you?"

"Maybe," I whispered.

"Unbelievable."

I drove down the driveway glancing back at the dog through the rearview mirror.

"He's magnificent."

"He certainly is," Rooster said. "Make a right."

I took one final look in the mirror then drove for about five miles until we saw roadside signs for a couple of motels. They were too far from the interstate to attract the interest of truckers, and I doubted if many tourists made their way here. I slowed as we approached the first motel that sat next to the road on our left. We scanned the empty parking spots in front of the rooms, and I accelerated. A few miles later, we approached the second motel that sat on our right, and Rooster pointed at a blue truck parked in front of the room on the far end of the small, weather-beaten structure.

"Definitely Walter's kind of place," Rooster said, reaching for his phone. "Pull over into that gas station." He called information for the main number of the motel then waited until the call went through. "Yes, hello. Could you please connect me with room twelve? Thank you." Rooster put his phone on speaker and waited.

"Hello?" said the confused voice on the other end of the line.

Rooster ended the call and slid his phone back into his pocket.

"You're pretty good at this stuff," I said, laughing. "How did you know the number of his room?"

"I counted to twelve," Rooster deadpanned.

"Smart aleck," I said, making a face at him. "How do you want to do this?"

"We're going to knock on his door, and then I'm going to knock some sense into him."

"A simple plan, but probably effective," I said, pulling back onto the road and heading for the motel. "I'll park somewhere near the office. We don't want to spook him."

Rooster nodded as he pulled on a pair of thick leather gloves. I turned the engine off and climbed out. We walked down the concrete path that fronted all the rooms and came to a stop near the door. Rooster nodded at me and hung back as I knocked. The door slowly opened halfway, and Coke Bottle peered out. It took his eyes a second to focus, then he recoiled when he recognized me.

"You?" he said, stunned. "What are you doing here?"

"Hi, Walter. At the moment, I'd like to come in out of the cold," I said, beaming at him.

"Not gonna happen," he said, starting to slam the door in my face.

Rooster blocked it with his foot, then shoved the door open hard, and we stepped inside. Coke Bottle stared in disbelief at Rooster, then toppled backward onto the bed when Rooster landed one of the hardest punches I'd ever seen thrown. I closed the door, and Rooster pointed at a chair in a corner. I sat down and stared in disbelief at the semi-conscious Coke Bottle who was bleeding from the nose and mouth.

"Get up," Rooster said, clenching and unclenching his fists.

"No, I don't think that's a good idea, Rooster," Coke Bottle said, cowering on the bed.

"Okay," Rooster said, approaching the bed. "Then stay right there." Rooster landed two more punches, and Coke Bottle rolled off the bed and fell onto the floor. Rooster bent down and lifted him by the shoulders and tossed him into a chair close to mine.

"Geez, Rooster," Coke Bottle said, blinking as he looked around the room for his glasses. "What did you do that for?"

"Because I forgot my gun, you moron," Rooster said, enraged. He bent down to pick up Coke Bottle's glasses, pushed them back into shape then handed them to his cousin. "Okay, start talking."

"About what?"

Rooster grabbed Coke Bottle by the hair and pulled it hard until Coke Bottle's head was bent back and the veins in his neck were pulsating. Then Rooster let go and pulled a chair directly in front of his cousin, turned it around, and sat down with his arms draped over the back of the chair.

"Don't make me ask you again, Walter," Rooster said in a voice that made the hairs on the back of my neck stand up.

"I'm down here looking for a dog," Coke Bottle said.

"A Tibetan Mastiff that goes by the name Chi?" Rooster said.

"I don't know his name," Coke Bottle said, shaking his head. "I mean, no."

Rooster reached out and grabbed one of his cousin's hands. Then he bent the pinkie finger back until I heard it pop. Coke Bottle howled and grabbed his hand as he stared at Rooster.

"Geez, Rooster," I said, grimacing. "Take it easy."

"One down, nine to go, Walter," Rooster said, ignoring me. "How many times have I told you to stay away from Clay Bay?"

"Uh, twice, I think," Coke Bottle whispered.

"And what happens when I have to tell you something three times?"

"Bad things."

"Suzy," Rooster said, glancing at me. "Grab that bag over there and have a look."

I got up, retrieved the large canvas bag and set it down on the bed. I began removing various items.

"We got a flashlight, a set of lock picks, a box of surgical gloves, a first aid kit, a bunch of specimen cups, and a small cooler packed with dry ice and what looks like a container of liquid nitrogen," I said, tossing the items on the bed. "Just what you need to keep everything nice and frozen." I removed the final item from the bag, stared at it, then strongly considered the possibility of using it on Coke Bottle. "A tranquilizer gun? You were going to shoot the Mastiff?"

"Well, I sure wasn't going to get my hands anywhere near him while he was awake," Coke Bottle said. "Have you seen the size of that dog?"

I tossed the gun on the bed and sat back down in my chair fuming, fully prepared to step in if Rooster decided he needed a break.

"How did you end up working for Sofia Rossi?" Rooster said.

"I did a couple of jobs for her dad a few years ago," Coke Bottle said. "He recommended me."

"When was this?" Rooster said.

"About three months ago."

"And your job is to steal dog semen?" Rooster said, staring at his cousin.

"Pretty much," Coke Bottle said with a shrug as he rubbed his damaged hand.

"Your mother would be so proud," Rooster said.

"Hey," Coke Bottle snapped. "Ms. Rossi pays me well. And it turns out that stuff is worth a fortune."

"What about the Otterhound?" I said.

"The otter what?" Coke Bottle said, staring at me.

At least, I think he was looking at me. Given the blood on his thick lenses and his constant blinking, it was a bit hard to tell.

"You didn't inseminate an Otterhound a couple of months ago?" I said.

"I don't have a clue what you're talking about, lady," he said, then glanced at Rooster. "Honest, Rooster. This is only my third job working for Ms. Rossi. The other two were an

Aza…wakh, and some dog from Turkey called a cattle something or other."

"Catalburun," I said. "They're one of the few dogs with a split nose."

"That's the one," Coke Bottle said. "When I first noticed the nose, I thought I might have screwed up and done something to it." He gave Rooster a pleading stare. "Honest, Rooster, I don't know nothing about no Otterhound."

Rooster stared at his cousin, then glanced over his shoulder at me.

"You believe him?" he said.

"Yeah, sadly, I think I do," I said, as my neurons began to churn and chart a new course.

"Okay," Rooster said, getting to his feet and walking toward the bed. He removed his gloves then fiddled with the clock that was sitting on the bedside table. "Suzy, I'm going to need you to wait in the car."

"What are you going to do, Rooster?" I said.

"Walter and I are going to have a little chat," Rooster said, sliding his gloves back on and rotating his head until his neck popped. "Go ahead, I won't be long."

"Rooster," I said, my voice rising in warning.

"Okay, stick around if you want. But I wouldn't recommend it."

"Rooster, just take it easy," Coke Bottle said. "I'll pack my stuff and get on the road back to Florida. I promise."

"Oh, I know you will, Walter. But you're probably going to need a couple hours to rest up. But don't worry, I just set the alarm for you. And I need to tell you that this is your final warning. Do you understand what I'm telling you?"

"I do."

"And after you take a little nap when we finish our *chat*, what are you going to do, Walter?"

"Drive straight to Florida."

"And if you don't?" Rooster said as if talking to a three-year-old.

"You're gonna call the cops?"

"You should be so lucky. Now, stand up."

"I don't think that's a good idea, Rooster. I'm a little woozy."

Rooster fired a punch I barely saw coming, and Coke Bottle rocked back in his chair. It teetered briefly, then toppled over.

"On second thought, I think I will wait in the car," I said, heading for the door.

"Good call," Rooster said, dragging his cousin to his feet.

I closed the door behind me and listened for about a minute before the thuds of Rooster's punches landing and Coke Bottle's whimpers sent me racing for the car. About five minutes later, Rooster climbed into the passenger seat and removed his gloves. He massaged his hands as he stared out the window.

"Are you okay?" I said.

"I'll be fine."

"I've never seen that side of you," I said, glancing over at him.

"I haven't shown it a very long time," he said, exhaling loudly.

"Was that really necessary?"

"Unfortunately, it's the only thing he listens to," Rooster said, running a hand through his hair.

"You think he's going to head back to Florida?"

"Oh, yeah. I'm positive."

Then he exhaled again and shook his head with a sad expression etched on his face.

"Family, huh?"

"Sure, sure."

*Chapter 18*

I walked into Chief Abrams' office and felt an overpowering blast of heat. The sudden temperature change was unbearable, and I unzipped and removed my coat. The Chief was sitting behind his desk deep in thought staring down at a Scrabble board. Freddie was across from him with his feet up on the desk and obviously anxious for the Chief to make his move.

"Hey, Snoop," Freddie said, gesturing at the chair next to his. "Have a seat."

"I thought you were going to Miami," I said, removing my wool toque as I sat down.

"I fly out tonight."

"What's going on with the heat? It has to be ninety in here," removing my scarf and tossing it on the desk.

"I think the thermostat is broken," the Chief said, not looking up from the board. "Billy is on his way down to take a look at it."

"C'mon, Chief," Freddie said. "Hurry up and make a play. I've got a meeting to get to."

"You do? When?" the Chief said, glancing up briefly with a frown.

"A week from Thursday."

"Funny," Chief Abrams said, placing four tiles on the board. "Okay, eerie. That's five points."

"Ten minutes to play eerie?" Freddie said.

"I'm consonant-challenged at the moment," the Chief said, sitting back in his chair. "What's up, Snoopmeister?"

"I thought I'd stop by and give you an update on our trip to Scranton," I said, watching as Freddie emptied his rack of tiles with a seven-letter word.

"Should I even bother to add that up, or do you surrender?"

"Unbelievable," the Chief said, pushing the board away. "Sure, let's hear the update. Anything is better than listening to him gloat. Did you find Coke Bottle?"

"We did," I said.

"And?"

"Rooster had a little chat with him," I said, deflecting.

"I'm sure he did," Chief Abrams said with a small grin. "And he's on his way back to Florida?"

"Yeah, I'd be shocked if he wasn't. But he was trying to steal dog semen. What a strange way to make a living."

"Maybe Coke Bottle just likes having a job where he can work with his hands," Freddie said, glancing over at me with a grin.

"Don't be disgusting," I said, glaring back at him. "Isn't there a dead body around you should be examining?"

"Thankfully, no," he said, placing his hands behind his head. "I wrapped everything up with Skitch Friendly yesterday, and I'm happy to report that everyone else is alive and well at the moment."

"Did you find a bullet in Friendly's shoulder?" I said.

"I did. Standard .30-06. And there's probably a thousand hunters around here who use that caliber. Why do you ask?"

"I just have this nagging feeling that Friendly's death wasn't an accident," I said.

"A feeling?" Freddie said.

"Yeah."

"Well, I guess that's all we need, right, Chief?" Freddie said, laughing.

"Shut it," I said, removing my sweater. "It's like a sauna in here."

"Did you ask Coke Bottle about the Otterhound?" the Chief said.

"We did. He said he didn't have a clue what we were talking about," I said. "And we believed him."

"Then I'm going to stick with my theory. Not that I agree with you that it wasn't an accident," the Chief said.

"Yeah, the lease rights," I said, nodding. "Oh, I forgot to tell you. We ran into Herman Billows a couple days ago when we were out at the Friendly's place."

"Did you tell him you were buying the property?" the Chief said, draping a leg over his knee.

"We did. And he wasn't very happy about it," I said, unbuttoning the top two buttons of my blouse.

"Should I put some music on?" Freddie said.

"What?" I said, staring at him.

"Well, if you're going to disrobe, I thought you might like to do it to music," Freddie said, grinning and shaking his shoulders. "You know, a little *boom, chicka-boom, chicka, boom-boom-boom.*"

"What is wrong with you?" I said, dumbfounded.

"Early winter funk, I imagine," he said with a shrug. "You should see me in February."

"I've seen you in February. And that's why I winter in Grand Cayman."

"So, what's your plan from here?" the Chief said after he'd stopped laughing.

"I have no idea," I said. "I'm stuck."

"That's probably because you're chasing ghosts on this one," the Chief said. "Sometimes things are just accidents."

"Yeah, you're probably right," I said. "Unless Billows tips his hand and gives us something to work with, I guess we'll just wait for the Otterhound to deliver then head to Cayman." Then my neurons flared. "But somebody inseminated that dog. It's driving me crazy."

"Try not to overthink it," the Chief said.

Freddie snorted. I shot him a dirty look but remained silent.

"Did your mom and Paulie get out?" the Chief said.

"Yeah, she called yesterday when they landed," I said. "She said they were going for a walk on the beach and then spend the rest of the day snuggling by the pool. It's eighty there today."

"Nice," the Chief said, glancing up at the clock on the wall. "Almost lunchtime. Do you know what Chef Claire is serving for today's special?"

"She's doing her stroganoff," I said, feeling my stomach rumble. "I'm heading over there from here. Want to join us?"

"Of course," the Chief said, getting up from his chair. "Who else is coming?"

"Just Rooster and Josie at the moment."

"Mind if I tag along?" Freddie said.

"You promise to behave yourself?" I said, cocking my head at him.

"You know I can't do that," he said, laughing.

"I'll see you guys there," I said, pulling on my sweater and scarf then my coat and hat and heading out the door.

Two minutes later, I met them in the parking lot behind the restaurant, and we entered through the back door. Chef Claire was in front of one of the stoves adding the final touches to a large pot. I picked up a strong whiff of wine and garlic as I approached to give her a hug.

"It smells fantastic," I said, peering into the pot.

"Yeah, I think it's going to be a good batch," Chef Claire said, waving to the men. "Hey, guys. How's it going?"

"Not as good as it's going to be in a few minutes," the Chief said, staring at the pot. "Are you serving it with the egg noodles?"

"I am," she said, stirring. "Rooster and Josie are in the lounge."

That was her nice way of saying *get out of the kitchen*, so I nodded for the Chief and Freddie to follow me.

"The door on the right," Chef Claire said without turning around.

"Everybody's a comedian," I said, heading for the lounge.

Josie and Rooster were sipping hot cider at the bar and chatting with Millie. I glanced around and waved to a small group of friends who were sitting in front of the fire. I sat down next to Josie and nodded at Millie when she held up a mug of the cider. I slipped my coat off then took a sip.

"How's Gabby doing?"

"She seems a bit closer today," Josie said. "But nothing yet."

"I guess the pups just aren't ready to come out," I said.

"In this weather, who can blame them?" Josie said, shrugging.

"Yeah. I'm so ready to get out of here," I said. "Oh, I completely forgot to mention something."

Josie swiveled her stool ninety degrees and waited for me to continue.

"My mother has decided against building the zoo behind the Inn."

"Good call on her part," Josie said, sipping her cider. "We've got more than enough on our plate as it is."

"Yeah," I said with a tentative frown.

"What?"

"My mom wants to turn the land over to us."

"Oh, I don't think I'm going to like where this is going," she said, setting her mug down on the bar.

"No, it's not bad," I said. "In fact, I kinda like the idea."

"What is it?"

"She wants us to expand," I said. "Turn the Inn into a regional operation, and open our services up to handle all sorts of different animals who are injured or need rescuing."

Josie rubbed her forehead as she gave it some serious thought. Eventually, she took another sip and exhaled.

"I guess my first question is why does she want to do that?"

"I'm not sure," I said. "But I think it might have something to do with her legacy."

"Can't she just give the library a couple hundred grand and ask them to put her name up in lights?"

I laughed loud enough to get the attention of everyone in the lounge.

"Gee, I don't know, Suzy," Josie said, shaking her head. "That would be a huge project. Not to mention what it would cost."

"She's offering to pay for it," I said. "If we agree to set it up as a non-profit."

"And put her name on it?" Josie said.

"That hasn't come up yet," I said, laughing. "But give her time."

"Between buying the Friendly's place to keep fracking out and setting up a regional rescue program, one might wonder if she's starting to put her affairs in order."

"That thought did cross my mind," I said, nodding.

"She's not sick, is she?"

"No, she's doing great," I said. "Healthy as a horse."

"Would she tell you if she wasn't?"

I thought about it for a long time then nodded.

"I'm sure she would."

"We'd need at least a couple more full-time vets. And a ton of new staff," Josie said.

"And be able to take care of a lot more animals," I said.

"Yeah, I do like that," she said, then shrugged. "Sure, why not? It's at least worth taking a look at."

"Okay, I'll let her know we want to talk to her about it when we get to Cayman," I said.

"Besides, we'll probably need the room," Josie said.

"What?"

"Rooster told me you were thinking about getting a Tibetan Mastiff puppy. Are you out of your mind?"

"You should have seen this dog," I said, beaming. "Magnificent."

*Chapter 19*

Josie left my office at eight to take the Otterhound's temperature, and a few minutes later she came back in and sat down on the couch. At least she did as soon as Captain and Chloe grudgingly conceded enough room.

"Her temperature has dropped two degrees," Josie said. "If it's the same in the morning, she's about ready."

Two consecutive readings of a lowered body temperature, twelve hours apart, almost always meant that labor would commence within twenty-four hours. My neurons flared briefly, and I started reviewing the checklist of what we needed to do to get ready.

"How's she doing?"

"She's fine. Just a little lethargic. But that's to be expected," Josie said, reaching into my desk drawer for a bag of bite-sized. She held it up to the light and frowned at me. "Really?"

"I've had a lot on my mind," I said, grabbing a small handful.

"She also started working on her nesting area," Josie said.

A few days ago, we'd put a large, low-sided wooden box in the corner of the Otterhound's condo and lined it with newspaper then laid some blankets on top. We knew the dog would instinctively create a safe and comfortable area where she could deliver her puppies and then spend most of her time in the nesting area while she waited for labor to begin.

"Did she eat her dinner tonight?" I said.

"She did not," Josie said.

"Okay, then I'm betting she's going to start delivering late tomorrow afternoon or early evening."

"Ten bucks she has her first puppy by five o'clock tomorrow," Josie said, popping a bite-sized.

"You're on," I said. "I'm going with no earlier than seven."

"I love taking your money. We might be in for a long night tomorrow," she said, glancing down at Captain who had begun to snore loudly. "Hey," she said, gently tapping his side. "We're trying to talk here."

Captain snorted, opened one eye, thumped his tail on the couch once, then went back to sleep.

We headed up to the house and spent the evening with Chef Claire and the dogs watching a movie before heading to bed. The next morning, the Otterhound's temperature was still two degrees lower than normal, and Gabby was restless and beginning to pant. Josie ran her stethoscope over the dog's stomach, then nodded with a big smile.

"Six little heartbeats pounding away," Josie said, sliding her stethoscope into her coat. "But I don't think she's producing milk yet."

"Is that a problem?"

"I don't think so," she said, shaking her head. "Some dogs don't produce until after they start whelping. But just to be on the safe side, why don't you grab some of the newborn puppy formula just in case she has any problems nursing?"

"It's her third litter," I said. "She's probably got this figured out by now, right?"

"That would be my guess," Josie said, stroking the dog's head. "What a good girl."

"Now, we wait," I said, getting to my feet. "You want to do shifts tonight?"

"No, I'm not missing this," Josie said, laughing.

"Me either."

We spent the rest of the day dividing our time between double-checking that everything was ready for our departure and keeping a close eye on Gabby. After the puppies were born, Josie and I planned to stick around until we were sure they and their mom were okay. Then Josie would perform the leg surgery. After we headed to Cayman, Sammy and Jill would have primary responsibility for the Inn and the puppies, and another vet who lived about an hour away would be on call as well as onsite three days a week. Five o'clock came and went, and when the clock hit six, Josie tossed a ten-dollar bill on my desk.

"Thanks," I said, holding the bill up. "I'm gonna have this one framed."

"Are you sure you guys don't need us to stick around?" Jill said, poking her head into the office.

"No, we'll be fine, Josie said. "It'll be just like the good old days when we used to do this sort of thing all the time."

"We don't mind," Sammy said, peering over Jill's shoulder.

"No, go home and enjoy your evening," I said, waving them off. "But if you don't feel like cooking tonight, Chef Claire is doing Tex-Mex up at the house."

"Really?" Sammy said, glancing at Jill. "What's she making?"

"Does it matter?" Josie said, laughing.

"No," Sammy said with a grin. "She won't mind?"

"She'll love having the company," I said. "But if you don't mind, take these two bruisers with you."

"Sure," Jill said. "Captain. Chloe. You ready to head up to the house?"

Both dogs glanced at us and stayed right where they were.

"Snack?" Jill said.

Captain and Chloe hopped off the couch and raced to the door.

"The magic word," Josie said.

"We'll bring you some dinner," Jill said, then closed the door behind her.

"Okay," Josie said, grabbing a fresh bag of bite-sized from my desk. "Let's do this."

We headed for the Otterhound's condo and sat down on either side of her. She was panting hard and seemed anxious. But she licked both our hands and produced a contented moan when Josie slowly ran her hand along her distended stomach.

At eight-thirty, the Otterhound stretched out on the nesting area and took a few minutes to find her most comfortable position. Soon after, the first puppy's head emerged.

"So far, so good," Josie said, watching the scene closely.

"This is always such an amazing thing to watch," I said, mesmerized by what I was seeing.

The first puppy emerged completely, and Gabby maneuvered her head next to the puppy. She gently tore the amniotic sac open, then bit the umbilical cord in half.

"She's a total pro at this," Josie whispered.

"Unbelievable," I said, shaking my head. "I want one of my own."

"A puppy?" Josie deadpanned.

"Shut it."

The Otterhound began licking the newborn puppy, and I watched for a couple of minutes. Then my mouth dropped open. I glanced at Josie who was also staring at the puppy, stunned.

"Now that's a game-changer," I said, my neurons on fire.

"So much for a litter of Otterhounds," she said, laughing. "Who do you think the father is?"

"It's probably going to take a few days to be sure, but I'm going to guess a Rottweiler by the name of Stinky."

"Sofia Rossi's dog?"

"Yup."

"How could she and Skitch Friendly let that happen?" Josie said. "They're going to be cute dogs, but they're sure not going to sell for big bucks."

"They obviously weren't paying close attention to what the dogs were doing," I said, rubbing my forehead.

"Because they were busy doing something similar with each other?" Josie said, glancing over at me.

"That thought did just cross my mind," I said, staring down at the puppy.

The Otterhound nuzzled the puppy close to her, and it soon began nursing. Then Gabby rested her head on the blankets as she waited for the next one to arrive.

"If they were having an affair, that certainly opens up a whole bunch of possibilities," Josie said. "I mean if you buy into the idea that Friendly's death wasn't an accident."

"It certainly does," I said, my mind racing.

"Rossi has an ex-husband, right?" Josie said.

"She does."

"And there's a good chance he could be mobbed up?"

"Given who her father is and the sort of business she's in, I'd say it's definitely a possibility."

"A jealous ex-husband with a rifle?" she said, gently stroking Gabby's head. "Good girl."

"I can see that," I said, nodding. "A stray bullet from a hunter. It would be logical to assume it was just an accident."

"So, instead of his death being tied into the leasing rights, we could be looking at jealousy as the motive?" Josie said, holding out the bag of bite-sized.

I waved the bag away and stared off into the distance. Then my neurons exploded, and I flinched.

"Don't do that," Josie said, startled and holding a hand to her chest. "What is it?"

"I don't think it's one or the other," I whispered.

"I'm going to need a little clarification, Suzy."

"I think it might be a bit of both."

# Chapter 20

By the time Gabby had finished delivering all six puppies, it was past midnight. Josie did an extensive examination of the Otterhound, pronounced that she and the puppies were all in great condition, then stood up and stretched.

"Good job," I said, staring lovingly at the sleeping puppies.

"We might be looking at a new breed," Josie said. "What should we call them?"

"Rotthound?"

"Not bad," she said, shrugging. "Otterweil?"

"Weilerhound," I said, nodding.

"Oh, I like that one," she said. "Okay, now that we've solved that, I'm going up for a shower, a snack, and bed in that order."

"Good plan. Lead the way."

I slept hard and dreamt deep and woke the next morning to the smell of bacon. I headed straight to the kitchen with my head pounding from an idea that had surfaced and begun to marinate just before I'd drifted off to sleep. I found Josie and Chef Claire in their pajamas sipping coffee along with four dogs who were on point and staring up at the frying pan on the stove. I greeted all four dogs then poured myself a cup of coffee and grabbed my phone as I sat down.

"Uh-oh, she's got that look," Chef Claire said, reaching for a handful of bacon.

"Yeah," Josie said, pouring maple syrup over her stack of pancakes. "She really shouldn't do that on an empty stomach."

"Shut it," I said, making a call. "Hey, Chief. Yeah, it is early. She did. Six beautiful puppies. What are you doing at the moment?...Well, instead of heading to the office, why don't you swing by the house and have breakfast with us? Pancakes and bacon...Great, we'll see you soon. Oh, would you mind stopping to pick Rooster up on your way?...I'll explain it all when you get here...Funny. Yes, you can eat first."

I set my phone down and reached for a plate.

"Rooster?" Josie said, frowning.

"I need his advice," I said, munching a slice of bacon. "You know, I think it might be a nice day to go cross-country."

Josie and Chef Claire stared at me, then at each other.

"Did she hit her head last night?" Chef Claire said.

"Not that I noticed," Josie said, then looked up from her pancakes. "Have you finally lost the plot?"

"Well, as bad as skiing is," I said, through a mouthful of pancake. "It sure beats trying to walk in that stuff."

"Okay," Josie said, shaking her head as she reached for the plate of bacon.

A few minutes later, Chief Abrams pulled into the driveway, and he and Rooster made their way up the driveway. I met them at the door and ushered them inside.

192

"Good morning," Rooster said.

"Thanks for coming," I said.

"Yeah, the Chief really had to twist my arm," Rooster said, sitting down in front of the plate of food Josie had created for him. "I was just about to make myself some toast."

"This looks fantastic, Chef Claire," the Chief said, rubbing his hands together.

"It's pancakes and bacon, Chief," she said, laughing. "Cool your jets."

"Yes, but it's your pancakes and bacon," he said, digging in.

"Aren't you sweet," she said, sitting back down to eat.

"Okay, Snoopmeister," the Chief said. "I know you didn't get me over here just to feed me. What's up?"

"I think I had a breakthrough last night."

"While the Otterhound was delivering?" the Chief said, frowning.

"Yeah, that's what started it," I said, digging into my stack of pancakes. "The puppies aren't purebred."

"They're not?" Rooster said, pausing just before he took a sip of coffee.

"No, they're mixed breed," I said. "And we're not sure yet, but one of the puppies looks a lot like a Rottweiler."

I paused and looked around to see if that little nugget of information registered with either of them.

"The Rossi woman has a Rottweiler, right?" Rooster said.

"She does."

"And you think her dog might be the father of the puppies?" the Chief said.

"I do."

"Good for the Rottweiler," the Chief said, staring at me. "And this matters why?"

"Horrible syntax, Chief," I said, frowning.

"Don't start," Josie said, adding some more maple syrup to her rapidly dwindling stack.

"I think Sofia Rossi and Skitch Friendly were having an affair," I said.

"That sounds like a major assumption on your part," the Chief said.

"Think about it," I said, my neurons firing on all cylinders as the coffee began to work its magic. "How could two people that interested in breeding rare dogs allow something like that to happen? They were both expecting a spring litter of Otterhounds. I think the dogs were left alone, and Skitch wasn't aware that Gabby was in heat."

"And they weren't paying attention to the dogs because they were busy doing other things?" Rooster said.

"Yes. And Sofia said that she had seen Skitch a couple of months ago," I said. "But she seemed coy about mentioning it, almost secretive."

"Well, he must have been to her place before because of what they were doing with the Otterhound," Rooster said. "And

Skitch did have a reputation as a player. But that was a long time ago."

"Before he decided to become a hermit?" I said.

"Yeah."

"He had a truck and loved to fish and trap. So, he must have been away from the cabin quite a bit," I said. "And since the rest of his family was stuck way out in the woods, there wasn't much chance he'd get caught cheating."

"You're right about that," Rooster said, frowning.

"So, your guess is that somebody figured out they were having an affair and decided to do something about it?" the Chief said, shaking his head. "I don't know. That sounds like a total stretch, Snoop."

"Maybe," I said.

"You said the Rossi woman was divorced," the Chief said. "Jealous ex-husband?"

I shook my head, and Josie stared at me.

"No?" she said.

"No," I said. "I don't think that's it."

"Then who?" the Chief said.

"A family member," I said, taking a sip of coffee.

"Not that goofy son of theirs?" the Chief said.

"Nope," I said. "Definitely not Cooter."

"The daughter?" Josie said.

"No," I said, shaking my head. "The widow Friendly."

"Jessie?" Rooster said, scowling. "No way."

"I agree. I have to say that I see a few holes in your theory," the Chief said.

"Only a few?" Rooster said, laughing.

I waited out the laughter by munching on a piece of bacon, then I took a sip of coffee, set my mug down and wiped my mouth. I leaned forward with both elbows on the granite island.

"Imagine you're a woman who's spent her adult life stuck out in the middle of the woods pretty much cut off from civilization. And you only agreed to live that way because you had devoted your life to your husband and were raising two kids. But then you found out he'd been cheating on you. And all the while, you're stuck living in the middle of nowhere chopping wood and tending a fire while he's off doing who knows what. I know that would certainly make my blood boil."

"Mine too," Josie said, nodding.

"Absolutely," Chef Claire said. "I'd be reaching for my softball bat."

"And you saw how quickly Jessie jumped on the idea of moving," I said to Rooster.

"She certainly did," he said. "But who the heck did she talk into shooting Skitch?"

"She didn't talk anybody into it," I said. "She did it."

"Okay, let's take a breath here," the Chief said. "Suzy, you're making a very serious accusation. It's one thing to say that she'd be furious if she found out her husband was cheating on her, it's something else altogether to accuse her of murder."

"I know that," I said, nodding. "But when we were at her place discussing the purchase of her property, she did something that I didn't give a second thought at the time."

"What was that?" Rooster said, staring at me.

"Remember when Cooter came into the cabin carrying the target he'd been shooting at?"

"I do."

"And then Jessie explained to him right away what he was doing wrong. Nobody would know how to make adjustments like that to a rifle scope if they didn't know their way around guns. Or how to shoot them. And she certainly had all the time in the world to practice out there."

"Yeah, I suppose she would," Rooster said. "And living way out there, it makes sense that she'd be good with a gun."

"And the first time we went out there, she was holding a shotgun," I said.

"There's still one major problem with your theory," the Chief said. "Skitch was out on the River trapping. That means he had their truck."

"Maybe she hid in the back," Josie said.

"But how did she get home?" the Chief said. "We had his truck in custody for a few days after we found his body."

"Never mind," Josie said, shrugging as she reached for a slice of bacon.

"That's way too far to walk," Rooster said.

"Maybe she got a ride," I whispered.

"From who?" the Chief said.

"Whom."

"Don't start," Josie said, laughing. "You were doing so well."

"Sorry."

"Okay, Snoop," the Chief said. "Who's the mystery person she got a ride with?"

"Herman Billows."

I glanced around as my comment hung in the air. The Chief scratched his head and frowned at Rooster who was also nonplussed.

"I think that Jessie found out about the affair, then Skitch told her that he had turned down Billows' offer. Between those two things, I think she might have just snapped. Then, perhaps with some encouragement from Billows, she decided that getting rid of her husband was her chance to get out of that cabin. And make a little money doing it by agreeing to sell the lease rights."

"But how did she find out about the affair?" Rooster said.

"My guess is that Billows told her," I said. "You and mom said that he had done some research on both of you before he made the offer on your land, right?"

"Yeah, we're sure he did," Rooster said. "He was pretty familiar with both of us right from the start."

"He probably did some digging into Friendly's life as well," I said. "And he somehow managed to text the daughter out of the blue. Do you know how long Billows has been hanging around?"

"I wouldn't have a clue," Rooster said. "But it shouldn't be that hard to find out. He must be staying nearby. Right, Chief?"

"I'm sure we could figure it out," the Chief said. "You think Billows might have followed Skitch one of the times he went to visit the Rossi woman?"

"Yeah, I think he might have."

"And then Billows told Jessie about the affair and offered her the lease deal. As well as agree to help her take out her husband," the Chief said.

"Yeah, that's what my neurons have landed on," I said.

"I gotta say, Snoop," the Chief said, shaking his head. "When you jump to a conclusion, you certainly go for the gold."

"The Russian judge gave her a 9.5," Josie deadpanned.

"Funny," I said, making a face at her.

"It's a fascinating theory," Chef Claire said.

"You really think so?" I said, glancing at her.

"I do. There's just one small problem," she said. "How on earth are you going to prove it?"

"I have no idea."

# Chapter 21

The question of how to prove my theory stuck with me through the rest of breakfast and continued to tug and nag at me as we headed down the path that led to the Inn. I held the back door open for everyone then followed them inside. Josie opened the door that led outside to the play area where the other dogs were playing tag and rolling around in the snow. Our four bruisers stared outside, then I swear they looked around at each other and shook their heads then headed toward the registration area. I led Chef Claire, Rooster and the Chief to the Otterhound's condo where Jill was sitting with her back against the wall keeping a close eye on mom and her sleeping puppies.

"How is everyone doing?" I said to Jill, who waved and smiled at us.

"They're great," Jill said. "The puppies just had breakfast and then dozed off. As soon as Gabby wakes up, I'm going to try to get some food in her. She's still pretty worn out."

"The little guy on the left definitely looks like he's got a lot of Rottweiler in him," Rooster said, peering into the condo.

"They're adorable," Chef Claire said. "How long will it be before we can play with them?"

"Long after we're in Cayman," I said as Josie approached the condo. "Unless it's absolutely necessary, we don't recommend that newborn puppies be picked up or played with until their eyes are open and they're walking around."

"It's usually around three weeks," Josie said, then glanced at Jill who was still sitting with her back against the wall near the nesting area. "Is everything good?"

"We're in great shape," Jill said, getting to her feet. "I've got a few things to take care of, but I'll swing back in about half an hour."

"No, that's fine, Jill," Josie said. "I'll keep an eye on them."

"I'll give you a hand," Jill said. "I love watching these little guys."

"She's as bad as the two of you," Rooster said, laughing.

"That's why we hired her," Josie said, giving Jill a quick hug as she exited the condo and headed to registration.

"Who's up for a little cross-country skiing?" I said.

Rooster and the Chief looked at each other.

"Let me guess, you want to go deliver the news to Jessie Friendly that the puppies have been born?" the Chief said.

"Sure, let's go with that," Rooster said, laughing.

"Well, she does need to know they're here," I said. "What do you say?"

"I'm in," Rooster said. "The last thing we need is you going out there unsupervised."

"I'm gonna pass," the Chief said. "Until we get a few facts put together, my going out there without a good reason would look pretty suspicious. I think I'll stick around here and see if I can have a little chat with Herman Billows."

"About what?" I said, raising an eyebrow at him.

"None of your business," the Chief said, laughing.

"Harsh," I said. "Are you going to ask him what he was doing the day that Friendly got shot?"

"Maybe," the Chief said. "If it comes up. At the moment, I'm more concerned about why he's so interested in getting lease rights for something that is currently banned in the State."

"Yeah, that still doesn't make a lot of sense," Rooster said. "But I guess his company is taking the long view that the ban will eventually be reversed."

"That's a long time to sit on something," the Chief said.

"Not for a monster of a company that size," Rooster said. "Those lease payments would be a drop in the bucket."

My neurons flared, and I flinched. Josie, startled, jumped back and dropped her bag of bite-sized. Individually wrapped morsels of chocolate and caramel delight scattered across the floor.

"Don't do that," Josie said, glaring at me as she bent down to pick them up. "What on earth is it now?"

"I was just wondering if Herman Billows might be blowing smoke up everybody's skirt," I said, motioning for them to follow me to my office.

I entered through the open door and found all four of our dogs sprawled out on the couch. They woke up when we came in, but didn't bother to move.

"Make yourselves comfortable," I said, shaking my head at the sight of them then sat down behind my desk and fired up my laptop.

Josie wiggled onto the couch, and Chloe and Captain grudgingly made room. Chef Claire whistled softly, and Al and Dente hopped off the couch. They jumped back up as soon as she'd sat down then occupied her lap. She sat quietly stroking their heads. Rooster and the Chief sat down on the other side of the desk. I waited impatiently for my laptop to fire up and drummed my fingers on the desktop.

"Please, stop," Josie said, nodding at my fingers.

"Sorry," I said, folding my hands together.

"She is loud, isn't she?" Chef Claire said, grinning at Josie.

"Between that and the flinching, I swear," Josie said.

"Shut it," I said, wiggling my fingers as the browser finally loaded.

"Can I ask what you're doing?" the Chief said.

"Sure, sure," I said, staring at the screen as I tried to come up with an appropriate search term. "Hey, Rooster?"

"Yeah."

"Did Billows ever actually send you a proposed contract for rights to your property?"

"I believe he emailed me something, but I didn't even bother to read it," he said, shrugging.

"Do you still have it?" I said.

"I'm sure I do," he said, reaching for his phone. "I never delete anything."

"Great. Can you email it to me?"

"Why?"

"Because I don't want to try to read a bunch of legalese in a four-point font on your phone," I said, frowning at him.

"Okay, hold your horses," Rooster said, then glanced at the couch. "Not only is she loud, but she can also be very annoying."

Josie and Chef Claire merely shrugged as Rooster emailed me the document. Seconds later, it appeared, and I opened the attachment.

"What are you looking for?" the Chief said.

"Wiggly legalese," I said.

"Must be a technical term," the Chief said, glancing at Rooster.

I searched the document for natural gas references and found three. But they appeared to be in sections of the document that pertained to general references about the operations of 3E and not directly related to the specific terms of the agreement.

"That's odd," I said, frowning.

"What is it?" Rooster said, getting up to look over my shoulder.

"The references to natural gas are pretty obscure," I said. "Let's try searching for lease rights."

"That's weird," Rooster said, staring at the screen. "There are lots of references to both those terms, but they don't show up together."

"No, they don't," I said. "Let's try *drilling* rights." I hit the enter key and waited. I stared at the screen. "Bingo." I highlighted the section and sat back in my chair. "Read that sentence."

"For the land outlined in Attachment 1, I hereby authorize 3E, and their authorized representatives, exclusive drilling rights, including all necessary means and methods of extraction and production readiness activities, for a period of forty years."

Rooster stared at the screen then shook his head.

"Isn't that what you'd expect it to say?" he said. "What am I missing?"

"The reference to exclusive drilling rights doesn't specifically mention natural gas," I said. "I'm no lawyer, but I read *exclusive* to mean they can drill for anything they want."

"Like what?" the Chief said.

"I have no idea," I said, then read from my screen. "But wouldn't all necessary means and methods of extraction and production readiness activities include mining?"

"I'm sure it would," Rooster said. "And there's certainly a lot of mining in this state."

"Yeah, there's no ban on that," the Chief said. "But what do we have around here? It's mostly sand and gravel, right? And some limestone."

"I think that's about it," Rooster said. "You occasionally hear about folks coming across some garnet and other gemstones, but nothing in any quantity."

I tapped another search term into the browser and waited for the results. I scrolled down the first page of results, then opened one. I read for several seconds, stared at the wall as my neurons surged, then continued reading. I sat back in my chair, concentrating hard.

"I think she's about to blow," Josie said to Chef Claire.

"Yeah, wait for it," she said.

"Wollastonite," I whispered.

"Wouldn't have got that with a million guesses," Josie said, shaking her head.

"What is that?" Chef Claire said, laughing. "The name of a band?"

"Funny," I said. "Have you guys ever heard of that before?"

Both Chief Abrams and Rooster shook their heads. I glanced at Josie and Chef Claire.

"Really?" Josie said. "You're asking me?"

"What is it?" Chef Claire said.

"Apparently, it's a mineral that forms in impure limestone."

"I've never heard of it," Rooster said. "What's it used for?"

"It looks like it has lots of industrial uses," I said, reading from the screen. "Plastics, ceramics, metallurgy. Friction products? What the heck are they?"

"Brakes, stuff like that," Rooster said.

"That's a list that sounds like something the military and folks in the space industry might be interested in," the Chief said.

"Yeah, it does," I said. "Don't rockets use a lot of ceramic tiles?"

"I believe they do," the Chief said. "It's all very interesting, Suzy, but why is this worth talking about?"

"Because New York produces one hundred percent of the Wollastonite in the country from four mines in the Adirondacks."

"Okay," the Chief said, nodding. "It's probably worth talking about."

"You think Billows might know there's a bunch of that stuff buried on our property?" Rooster said.

"I don't know," I said. "Could a geological survey identify something like that?"

"Given the fact that the government can read my license plate from outer space, I'm gonna go with yes," Josie said, popping a bite-sized.

"But if that's the case, why haven't we ever heard about it before?" Rooster said.

"Maybe nobody has ever really looked for it around here," I said. "Since all the known reserves are in the Adirondacks."

"Maybe they're running out of it," Josie said. "You know, they might have dug up most of what's there."

"Does 3E have a sister company that's involved in defense contracting?" the Chief said.

"You're on fire today, Chief," I said, laughing as I typed. "That's a great idea."

"I have my moments," he said, shrugging.

"Bingo," I said, scanning the landing page of the company's website. "They certainly do."

"So, they sent Billows up here ostensibly to get natural gas rights but failed to mention that they also want to mine that stuff?" Rooster said.

"I think it's possible," I said. "And Billows probably assumed nobody knew what they were sitting on."

"And thought he was dealing with a bunch of country bumpkins," Josie said.

"Oh, I hate when that happens," I said, laughing. "And I bet his company was throwing smoke at other companies by only talking about natural gas rights. If this Wollastonite is valuable, they might not have wanted to let their competitors know what they're up to."

"It sounds like an awful lot of subterfuge to go through," Chef Claire said. "Couldn't they just get that stuff from another supplier? There must be other countries that have it."

"I'm sure they could," the Chief said. "Unless it would be a lot cheaper to dig their own supply from here."

"Or they don't want anybody knowing about some of the things they're using it for," Rooster said.

"Weird," Chef Claire said, shaking her head. "I'm so glad I spend all my time around dogs and food." She glanced around the office. "So, are we going skiing or not?"

"We are," Rooster said, getting to his feet.

"I'm out," Josie said, getting up off the couch. "I have some puppies to keep an eye on."

"If we're right about this, would that change your mind about signing with Billows?" I deadpanned. "It could be worth a fortune."

"Are you out of your mind?" Rooster said, scowling at me. "I don't give exclusive rights to anything or anybody."

"Just checking," I said, beaming at him.

# Chapter 22

With me in the middle of a relatively straight line, we trekked through the fresh snow. It was cold, but the sun was shining bright, and we were all wearing sunglasses. An anomaly, perhaps, to those unfamiliar with the overpowering glare that sunlight and pure white snow produce, but you can take my word for it that the sunglasses were more of a necessity than a fashion statement. But Chef Claire in her one-piece ski outfit and reflector glasses looked fantastic, and I suppressed a chuckle when I caught Rooster's furtive glance at her.

"You old dog," I whispered to him.

"What?" he said, not breaking stride.

"Enjoying the view?" I said, laughing.

"Hey, I'm old, not dead."

I was still sore from my last journey aboard the two narrow strips of fiberglass that looked a lot better hanging on the garage wall than they did attached to my feet. But since I was on a mission of discovery, my mind was focused on things other than my aching back and legs, and I was determined to not only do my best to keep up with Rooster and Chef Claire but also keep my complaints to a minimum. Sadly, the paths our skis had carved the other day were long gone, now buried by close to a foot of fresh snow that continued to fall.

"So, how do you want to play this?" Rooster said.

"I thought we'd start by telling Jessie about the puppies and see what sort of reaction we get," I said between gulps of fresh air. "And we'll just play it by ear from there."

"Okay," Rooster said, then glanced over at me and noticed my discomfort. "You need a break?"

"No, if I stop, I'll never start again," I said, looking over to my right at Chef Claire. "How are you doing?"

"Great," she said, beaming at me. "It's beautiful out here. So peaceful and relaxing."

"Relaxing?" I whispered as I shook my head. I turned toward Rooster. "She's a freak of nature."

"You'll get no argument from me," Rooster said, watching Chef Claire effortlessly work her way through the snow.

"What?" Chef Claire said, glancing over at us.

"Nothing," I said, commanding my lungs to take in more air.

A few minutes later, we reached the edge of the fence that surrounded the Friendly's cabin, and I came to a stop and looked around. If I'd been watching what stretched out in front of me on TV, I'd probably be oohing and aahing at the idyllic scene. But since I was standing in the middle of it in the wind and cold and a half-inch of fresh snow already covering my head and shoulders, my verbal expressions were somewhat more tempered.

"Language," Rooster said, frowning at my latest outburst.

"Sorry," I said, doing my best to fend off a leg cramp. I removed both skis, leaned them against the fence then glanced back and forth at my two fellow skiers. I removed the squirrel hat from my pocket and pulled it on over the toque I was wearing. I cocked my head and struck a pose for them.

"What do you feed that thing?" Chef Claire said, laughing.

"Smart aleck chefs," I said, adjusting the collection of dead squirrels that actually fit much better when I was wearing the knitted hat underneath.

"You guys ready?"

"I am," Chef Claire said with an expression that was a mixture of wonder and disbelief.

"What is it?"

"I'm just having a hard time believing anybody could actually live out here," Chef Claire said. "No running water or electricity, right?"

"Nope," Rooster said. "C'mon let's get inside. I could go for a glass of Jessie's shine."

"She makes her own moonshine?" Chef Claire said, following Rooster through the gate he was holding open. "This just keeps getting better. I should probably warn you guys that if I hear banjo music, I'm gonna freak out."

Rooster and I laughed as we headed across the front yard. The front door opened, and Jessie Friendly stepped out onto the porch and waved. We walked up the steps and brushed and stamped the snow off before following the widow into the cabin.

Very and Cooter hopped to their feet when they saw us and smiled.

"Hey, look who's here," Very said. "What brings you out on a day like this?"

"We've got some news about Gabby and the puppies," I said. "I don't think you've met Chef Claire before."

"It's nice to meet you," Very said.

"Same here," Chef Claire said, smiling. "I'm sorry I didn't get a chance to say hello when you were in the restaurant the other night."

Very frowned and lowered her head. Then she caught the look her mother was giving her.

"What is she talking about, Very?"

Very, caught red-handed, shrugged.

"I snuck out the other night," Very said. "I had a date."

"With the Billows fellow, right?" Jessie said.

"Yes, Mama."

Jessie continued to stare at her daughter, then nodded.

"Well, I guess you might as well get started adjusting to normal life," she said. "I just wish you would have told me. Now that your father's gone, you don't have to go sneaking around anymore."

"Thanks, Mama," Very said, giving her mother a small smile.

"Hi, Suzy. The hat looks great on you."

"Hey, Cooter," I said. "It fits a lot better when I wear the toque underneath."

"I could make you a smaller one," Cooter said. "I've got a new batch of skins drying in the barn."

"No, that's okay," I said. "This one is just fine."

"Can I get you folks something to drink?" Jessie said. "Rooster, I know you won't say no to a glass of shine." Then she focused on Chef Claire. "How about you?"

"I'd love to try it," Chef Claire said.

"Suzy?"

"I'll stick with coffee if you have it," I said.

Jessie headed into the kitchen and soon returned with our drinks. She gestured at the sitting area, and all six of us sat down.

"I take it that Gabby had her litter," Jessie said.

"She did," I said, smiling at the memory of the night they'd been born. "Six gorgeous puppies."

"I guess it'll be awhile before we're able to pick them up, right?" Jessie said, taking a sip of shine.

"Yes," I said. "But I need to tell you that they're not purebred Otterhound."

Jessie stared at me, confused by the news.

"They're not?" she said. "Then what the heck are they?"

"We're pretty sure the father was a Rottweiler," I said.

"Rottweiler?" Jessie said with a frown. "Where the heck did she come in contact with a Rottweiler?"

"You don't know?" I said.

"No," she said, taking another sip. "Cooter, have you seen any stray dogs around the past few months?"

"No, Mama."

"Me either," Very said, shaking her head.

"They're beautiful puppies," I said.

"But not rare or valuable, right?" Jessie said.

"No, from a monetary standpoint, I'm afraid not," I said.

"A Rottweiler?" Jessie said. "That's odd. I don't know what we'd do with six puppies. Especially since we'll probably be right in the middle of moving to Florida."

"We'll take care of the puppies," I said. "Don't worry about that. What about Gabby?"

"I'm taking Gabby," Cooter said. "She loves it out here, and I can use the company."

"Perfect," I said, nodding.

"And I wouldn't mind taking a couple of the puppies," Cooter said. "We got tons of room."

"Are you sure you want to do that, Cooter?" Jessie said.

"Yes, Mama," Cooter said. "Gabby can use some company too."

"Okay," Jessie said, smiling at her son. "C'mon, Very. Our guests look hungry. Give me a hand in the kitchen."

"Is there any way you can get into town at some point so you can pick out which puppies you'd like?" I said.

"I'll figure out a way," Cooter said.

"Good," I said. "It looks like your mom and Very are excited about moving."

"They are," Cooter said, nodding.

"How about you?" I said. "Are you going to be okay living out here all by yourself?"

"Yeah," he said. "I'm looking forward to finally getting some peace and quiet."

I glanced at Rooster and Chef Claire who looked back at me and shrugged. I guess what some people consider peace and quiet is relative. Then my neurons flared briefly.

"Have you met Herman Billows?" I said.

"Sure," Cooter said, nodding. "He's been out here a couple of times since Papa died. And I met him the first time he was here."

"The first time?" I said. "When was that?"

"It was a couple of weeks ago. He just showed up one day and tried to talk Papa into signing over lease rights to some gas that's sitting on our property." Cooter gave us a wide grin. "You should have seen the way Papa ran him off as soon as he figured out why he was here."

"I'm sure that was a sight," Rooster said with a grin.

"Yeah, the guy hightailed it out of here when Papa started toward the gun rack and told him he could shoot the…rear end out of a raccoon from a thousand yards."

"Did you get a chance to talk to Mr. Billows?" I said.

"Yeah, I had to keep him company for quite a while until Papa finished up what he was doing in the barn," Cooter said. "I had to do it since Mama and Very weren't here."

"They weren't?" I said, frowning.

"No, they were in town picking up some stuff," Cooter said. "I think Mama needed sugar for a fresh batch of shine."

"What did you talk about?" I said.

"Rocks, mostly," Cooter said, shrugging. "When he got here, I was polishing some rocks on the porch."

"I see," I said, glancing at Rooster. "Interesting."

"Yeah, Mr. Billows really likes rocks. He asked me to show him my collection, so I did. I even gave him one as a present. And he was so impressed with them, he asked me if I'd show him where I got them from."

"You didn't just find them on the ground?" I said, my neurons flaring.

"Don't have to," Cooter said. "We've got a whole cave of them."

"A cave?" I said.

"Yeah, in the woods behind the house," Cooter said. "It's a beautiful cave. Actually, it's a whole bunch of them."

"I'd love to see it," I said.

"Me too," Rooster said.

"Then come on," Cooter said, giving us a big grin as he stood up. "I'll go grab some flashlights and a couple of lanterns and meet you on the porch."

He grabbed his coat and headed out the back door. We watched him go then Rooster and I looked at each other.

"A cave. You think Billows recognized what was in there?" Rooster said.

"I'm counting on it," I said, then glanced at Chef Claire who had her legs tucked underneath her on the couch as she sipped her moonshine. "You want to come along?"

"After half a glass of this stuff, the last thing I need to be doing is crawling around a cave," she said. "I think I'll just sit right here. And maybe have another one."

"Be careful with that stuff," Rooster said. "It sneaks up on you in a hurry."

# Chapter 23

Cooter led us through a thick stretch of woods that had Rooster and I regularly stepping around or under low hanging pine boughs heavy with snow. About a quarter mile from the house, I got a stitch in my side but said nothing as Cooter led us past a series of boulders that were partially buried in the snow. Thankfully, he stopped moments later and pointed at a large rock formation that rose about fifty feet above the ground.

"The entrance is right over here," Cooter said, carefully making his way through the snow.

"You could have fooled me," I said, looking around the immediate area.

"Take your time," Cooter called out over his shoulder. "And watch where you're walking. There's a couple of spots where the snow has covered up some holes in the ground."

I nodded as I took another step and my leg disappeared from sight as I sunk into the snow up to my waist.

"Smooth," Rooster said, chuckling as he grabbed my hand and pulled me out.

"How do they live out here?" I said, brushing myself off.

"I imagine you get used to it. The early settlers certainly figured out a way to deal with it."

"Good for the early settlers."

"Over here," Cooter said, waving at us.

We made our way through a four-foot drift, and I frowned at a small opening in the rock formation.

"That's the entrance?" I said.

"Yeah, it's pretty small and easy to miss," Cooter said, dropping to his knees to brush the snow away from the opening. "But don't worry, it opens up once you get inside."

"Don't worry, it opens up once we get inside," Rooster said, glancing at me.

"Yeah, I heard him," I said, making a face at him.

"You're not claustrophobic, are you?" Rooster said, dropping to his knees.

"Only when I'm in confined spaces," I said, staring at the narrow opening.

"Funny," Rooster said, crawling through the opening. "Keep that sense of humor handy. I have a feeling we might need it."

"I really wasn't going for funny, Rooster," I said, crawling through the snow until I reached the entrance.

I spent the next several moments on my hands and knees in complete darkness dealing with the onset of a panic attack, then a beam of light hit me in the eyes. I waved it away, then shielded my eyes.

"Just a couple more feet," Cooter said, moving the beam to my right. "There you go. You can stand up now."

I climbed to my feet and followed the beam of light as Cooter shined it around the confined space. My breathing was shallow, and I grabbed Rooster's hand hard.

"Ow," he said. "I'm gonna need that, Suzy."

"Just as soon as I'm done with it," I said, squeezing hard as I started to hyperventilate. "I don't think I can do this."

"Hang in there," Rooster said. "Say, Cooter, would you mind lighting those kerosene lamps?"

"Sure, Rooster."

Moments later, the area just inside the entrance was bathed in dim light. I looked around the space that was circular and about twenty feet wide. The ceiling was about ten feet high, and I heard the sound of trickling water.

"Cooter, are you sure there's enough air in here?" I said, fighting the urge to turn and run.

"I've got plenty," he said, setting one of the lanterns on a nearby rock. "Are you running out?"

"Of the cave?" I said. "The thought has crossed my mind."

"No, I meant running out of air," Cooter said.

"Oh, that. No, not yet. I was just checking," I said, taking a deep breath and filling my lungs with stale air. "What's that smell?" I said to Rooster.

"Guano."

"Bats?" I said, squeezing his hand again.

"Technically, it's bat crap," he said, glancing up at the ceiling.

"There are bats in here?"

"I'd be very surprised if there weren't," he said, pointing at something dark hanging from the ceiling.

"Perfect," I said, glancing back at the entrance. "Okay, nice cave. Thanks for showing it to us, Cooter."

"You haven't seen anything yet," Cooter said, motioning for us to follow him. "Come on."

"I don't like this, Rooster."

"Hey, you're the one who raised their hand."

"Yeah, I really need to start working on that."

We followed Cooter for about fifty feet down an incline, then he came to a stop. He handed us flashlights, and I immediately switched mine on. I scanned the section of the cave we were now in and noticed that it was definitely starting to open up.

"Okay, before we go any further, I need to tell you a couple of things you'll want to remember," Cooter said.

"You got anything to write with?" I said to Rooster.

"Shhh," he said, laughing. "Just pay attention."

"The cave floor gets slippery in spots," Cooter said. "And you never know when it's going to happen so watch where you're going."

"Okay, got it. Baby steps it is," I said, committing the safety tip to memory.

"And you might hear the sound of animals from time to time," Cooter said.

"Animals? What kind of animals?" I said, frowning.

"Only animals that can fit through the entrance," Cooter said.

"Well, that makes me feel so much better," I said, agitated. "We just fit through the entrance, Cooter."

"Don't worry, they're more scared of you than you are of them," he said.

"Not to belabor the point, Cooter, but that sounds a lot like the last words of someone who was just eaten by a bear."

Cooter laughed.

"Belabor. You're funny."

"Why does everyone think I'm going for funny?" I said, surveying the immediate area with my flashlight.

"I'm sure there aren't any bears in here," Cooter said. "But you might see the occasional fox or coyote. And I have crossed paths with a skunk before. That was a bad day."

"Okay, point two," I said, shaking my head at Rooster. "Be on the lookout for wild animals. Is there anything else?"

"Just one more," Cooter said. "And this is the *really* important one."

"Are you listening?" Rooster whispered. "This is the really important one."

"Oh, don't worry, I'm rapt."

"We're gonna go about a hundred feet forward," Cooter said, pointing his flashlight. "And then we're going to come to a bigger cave."

"Got it," I said, listening closely. "A hundred feet ahead. Big cave."

"And we'll walk across it and then the path is going to form a Y," Cooter said. "The one on the right will lead us into another section of caves that goes a really long way. You can spend hours exploring and not see the same thing twice."

"Where does the one on the left go?" I said, frowning.

"Down."

"Down?"

"Yeah. It goes straight down."

"How far down?" I said.

"Probably seven or eight Mississippi," Cooter said, shrugging. "But I'm a fast counter."

I thought back to my problem of going out the wrong kitchen door at the restaurant and was positive I wouldn't be making the same mistake here.

"I've dropped rocks down there and counted," Cooter said. "And they always land with a splash."

"Must be an underground spring," Rooster said. "Has anybody ever gone down there?"

"Not that I know of," Cooter said, shaking his head.

"That would be something to see," Rooster said. "We could probably set up a system of ropes and pulleys and climb down."

"Are you out of your freaking mind?" I said, staring at him.

"Where's your sense of adventure?" Rooster said, laughing.

"I'm standing in the middle of a cave that's infested with wild animals in the dead of winter. What more do you want?"

"Well, look who's here."

All three of us turned around when we heard the voice and saw Herman Billows standing about ten feet behind us.

"What the heck are you doing here?" Rooster said.

"Just protecting my interests," he said, turning off the flashlight he was holding. "I stopped by to have another chat with the widow Friendly and saw you folks heading this way."

"This is unbelievably weird," I said to Rooster.

"When the going gets weird, the weird turn pro," he said, staring at Billows.

"Who said that?"

"Hunter S. Thompson," Rooster said.

"That's right," I said. "Interesting guy."

"Yeah, he probably would have enjoyed this particular moment of weird."

"So, you just want to purchase the property so you can leave it untouched, huh?" Billows said, rocking back and forth on his feet.

"Yeah, that's the plan," I said.

"Nice try, Suzy," Billows said. "Do I look like I just fell off the turnip truck?"

"Rhetorical, right?" I said to Rooster.

"Nothing gets past you."

"When my bosses sent me up here, I said sure. How hard can it be to negotiate with some bumpkins about lease rights that could make them rich?" Billows said. "It's tough enough handling Jethro here and the rest of the Clampetts. But little did I know I'd be dealing with you two and that overbearing enchantress you call your mother."

"Hey, knock it off," I snapped. "I'm the only one who can talk about my mother like that."

"Overbearing enchantress isn't bad," Rooster said, laughing. "You gotta give him that."

"Yeah, I need to remember that one."

"My name is Cooter, not Jethro."

"Unbelievable," Billows said, shaking his head. Then he nodded at my head and laughed. "Nice hat."

"What's wrong with it?" Cooter said, frowning.

"Now *that* is what I call a rhetorical question," Billow said, still laughing.

"Why are you making fun of Suzy's hat?" Cooter said. "Stop it."

"Okay, Jethro, whatever you say."

"Why are you here?" I said.

"I'm here making an offer to buy the property," Billows said. "If you think I'm going to let you slink in here and buy it out from under us, you're out of your mind."

"Slink?" I said to Rooster. "Did we slink in today?"

"No, it was more of a trudge."

"Yeah, that's the word for it," I said, then focused on Billows. "So, now you want to buy the property instead of just leasing the rights?"

"As soon as I got a look at this place and had the rock Jethro gave me analyzed, things changed," Billows said, staring around the cave.

"And you're willing to outbid us?" Rooster said.

"Up to a point," Billows said. "But we're certainly willing to keep upping our offer to where it's going to hurt you to write that check. And we're prepared to pay until it stops making financial sense to go any further. It's your lucky day, Jethro. You're going to be a rich man."

"I'm confused," Cooter said. "What's he talking about, Suzy?"

"He's talking about something called Wollastonite," I said, glaring at Billows.

"Woola what?"

"It's a mineral that's found in some of the rocks in this cave," I said.

"You've done your homework. Well done. So, you have been trying to scam us out of the deal," Billows said, nodding. "I knew it."

"Suzy?" Cooter said, giving me a wide-eyed stare.

"Cooter, Mr. Billows' company would like to buy your land so they can have what's in here."

"And do what with it?" Cooter said, frowning.

227

"This guy is too much," Billows said, laughing and shaking his head. "We're going to mine it, Jethro."

"You want to start digging in the ground?" Cooter said. "In here?"

"Well, we're sure not going to be spelunking," Billows said, exasperated. "We'll start digging in here and see where it leads. If this cave system is as big as you say it is, who knows how much we'll find."

"How pure was the sample you had tested?" Rooster said.

"You wouldn't believe it," Billows said, grinning. "We might be looking at one of the purest veins ever discovered."

"He's talking about digging up some of our property?" Cooter said.

"He's talking about digging up all of it," Rooster said.

"But I live here," Cooter said. "You can't do that."

"Maybe you'll get lucky, and your buddies here will bail you out. But it's probably going to cost them millions to do it," Billows said. "Sorry, folks. But it's time to play a little corporate hardball."

"Millions?" Cooter said, his eyes wide. "Are you talking about millions of *dollars*?"

"Well, I'm sure you'd rather be dealing in squirrel skins," Billows said, laughing. "But I doubt if I could get that past the lawyers." Then he looked at my hat again and shook his head. "That thing just cracks me up."

A strange look came over Cooter's face, and his demeanor changed immediately.

"If you're talking about millions of dollars, I guess that changes things," Cooter said, nodding. "I can always buy another place to live."

"Cooter?" I whispered.

"I know what I'm doing, Suzy," Cooter said, staring at me. "And it's not your property yet."

"No, you're right, it's not," I said, studying his expression.

"Well, if you're looking for a place to start digging," Cooter said, pointing at the cave behind us. "You're going to want to start in there. Follow me."

Billows switched his flashlight on and stepped past us with an evil grin as he followed Cooter's path. Rooster and I trailed close behind.

"The kid is selling out for big money?" Rooster whispered.

"It certainly looks that way," I said, then my neurons flared. "Uh-oh."

"What?" Rooster said, then shook his head and stared at me. "No. No way. You think so?"

"I do," I said, stepping into a larger cave.

Cooter was talking and pointing out different sections of the cave with the beam from his flashlight. Billows was listening closely and nodding. Rooster and I followed them to the other side of the cave and onto the pathway that soon formed a Y.

Cooter motioned behind his back for us to stay away as he took a few steps forward.

"The path on the right doesn't go very far," Cooter said. "But you won't believe what you see on this side."

"We need to stop him," Rooster whispered.

"Absolutely," I said, then called out. "Cooter, why don't you show Mr. Billows the path on the right?"

"I know what I'm doing, Suzy," Cooter said, then caught himself. He thought for a moment then nodded. "Yeah, maybe you're right. Come on, Mr. Billows. Let me show you the other path."

"No, it's quite alright, Jethro. I've got this." Then he glanced at Rooster and me over his shoulder. "And you two can just keep your nose out of it," Billows said, taking a step down the path on the left. "You've already caused enough problems as it-Aaaaaaaahh!"

I silently counted as we waited for the splash. When it finally came, it was faint but echoed softly throughout the cave.

"How far did you get?" I said to Rooster.

"Five Mississippi."

"Yeah, me too."

"What are we going to do now?" Rooster said, staring at Cooter who was standing at the edge of the hole peering down into the darkness.

"You mean about Cooter?"

"Yeah," Rooster said. "Technically, he sort of killed the guy."

"I guess that's one way of looking at it," I said, frowning. "But it's not like he pushed him."

"No, he didn't do that," Rooster said. "And he did try to talk him out of it."

"Yes, he did."

"But still."

"Yeah, I know," I whispered. "I'm gonna need a few minutes to process this."

"I'm gonna need another glass of Jessie's shine," Rooster said, shaking his head.

"I think I might join you," I said. "Hey, Cooter, you about ready to head back to the cabin?"

"Yeah, we probably should get going," he said, taking a final look down the hole before walking toward us. "How much trouble am I in?"

"I don't know, Cooter," I said. "I really don't know."

We followed Cooter back the way we came in, and just as we were about to reach the entrance, we heard the sound of someone coming into the cave. I stared in disbelief when Chief Abrams got to his feet and brushed the snow off.

"Wow," I said, stunned. "What on earth are you doing here?"

"If you answered your phone once in a while you'd know," Chief Abrams said, glaring at me.

"A little snarky, Chief. There's no reception out here," I said. "Why were you trying to call me?"

"Because I've been following Billows all morning. And as soon as I figured out where he was going, I thought I'd give you a heads up. When I got here, I saw him heading this way and followed him. Where is he?" the Chief said, glancing around.

"Uh, he fell down," I said, glancing at Rooster.

"So, he's hurt and lying down somewhere back in there?" the Chief said, staring into the distance.

"Actually, he fell *down*," Rooster said, pointing at the ground.

"Really?" the Chief said. "How far down?"

"Five Mississippi," Rooster and I said in unison.

The Chief frowned and glanced back and forth at us. Then his expression turned quizzical.

"So, you're telling me Billows had an *accident*?"

"Well, I'm sure he didn't do it on purpose," I said, glancing at Rooster.

"No, you're right about that," Rooster said. "He definitely didn't jump or anything like that."

"And he certainly wasn't pushed," I said, staring down at the floor. "And Cooter tried to warn him."

"I did," Cooter said, vigorously giving us his best bobblehead. "But he didn't listen."

"No, he didn't," I said, having a hard time making eye contact with Chief Abrams.

The Chief studied our faces, and I'm sure we looked like three schoolkids caught doing the wrong thing in the wrong place at the wrong time. Then he nodded and kept whatever was going through his head to himself.

"Okay, so Billows had an accident and did a header down a deep hole," he said. "Is there any chance he's still alive?"

"I'm gonna go with no," I said after a long pause.

"Yeah, me too," Rooster said. "That was an awfully long way to fall."

"Five Mississippi," I said, shrugging as I flashed the Chief a tentative smile.

"Okay," the Chief said, nodding. "Let's get out of here. I need to get a rescue crew out here to recover his body."

"Any chance I can go with you?" Rooster said.

"You want to go down that hole?" the Chief said, staring at Rooster.

"Yeah, I wouldn't mind taking a look," Rooster said.

"You're even weirder than she is," the Chief said, nodding at me as he turned and crawled back outside through the small opening.

"Thanks for helping me out," Cooter said after the Chief had disappeared from sight.

"Don't mention it," Rooster said, staring hard at Cooter. "To anybody."

# Chapter 24

Cooter and Rooster headed back to the cabin while I took Chief Abrams to the spot Very had shown me where his phone would work. As soon as his call went through, I waved and trudged back toward the cabin. I was freezing, but my mind was racing with other thoughts, and the cold was way down my list of concerns. As far as the fate of Herman Billows was concerned, I was again stunned by how quickly a life can end. And I was also conflicted about Cooter's actions as well as our complicity in covering for him. I decided Cooter had simply panicked when he realized that his beloved homeland might soon become an enormous quarry, overrun with earthmoving equipment, and his hunting and fishing areas destroyed.

And the fact that Billows had made fun of my hat probably hadn't helped.

Rooster and I needed to discuss the ramifications of our providing cover for a simple-minded but gentle soul whose primary desire was to be left alone to live a solitary life. I assumed Cooter's battle on that front wasn't over since there was a good chance that Billow's company would send another emissary making an offer Jessie Friendly might have a hard time turning down. And while my mother and Rooster would initially put up some degree of resistance, I was certain they wouldn't participate in a bidding war for the property. And as far as I was concerned, I had less interest in fighting a corporate conglomerate for ownership of the land than I did in following Rooster down a five Mississippi hole in the ground.

As I neared the cabin, my thoughts returned to Skitch Friendly's death, and I found myself doing a 180 reversal and somehow managed to convince myself that no one in the family had been responsible. I could make a case that Jessie and Very, given their speedy decision to basically take the money and run, both had enough of a motive. But it was impossible to miss the sad reverence in their eyes and voices every time his name came up, and I was no longer even sure that Jessie knew anything about her husband's affair. And I was left with the idea that fate had dealt the hand they were playing, and the two women were merely taking advantage of an opportunity to make their lives easier and begin building fresh memories.

In short, I was once again in agreement with the official story that Skitch Friendly's death had been an accident. I guess the Chief and my mom are right: Sometimes the facts just speak for themselves.

I approached the cabin and noticed Chef Claire sitting on the front porch. I climbed the steps and sat down next to her.

"What are you doing sitting out here in the cold?"

"Trying to sober up," Chef Claire said, staring off into the distance. "I'm hammered."

"How many glasses did you have?"

"Just two. That stuff is brutal," she said, shaking her head.

"Maybe she'll give you the recipe," I said, laughing.

"Yeah, that's all I need," she said, exhaling loudly.

"Did you hear what happened?"

"I did," Chef Claire said. "What a way to go, huh?"

"Yeah."

"Caves are dangerous places," she said, slurring her words. "Just an accident waiting to happen."

"Yeah, an accident," I whispered, then stood up. "I'm freezing. You coming?"

"I'll be in soon."

I headed inside and removed my coat and boots and both hats. Rooster was sitting on a couch talking with Jessie. I sat down across from them.

"Where's Very and Cooter?"

"Cooter's upset about what happened, and Very went to his room to see if she can calm him down," Jessie said. "What a horrible thing to see. That poor boy." She looked around and shrugged. "And I can't imagine it was much better for you two."

"Yeah, it was quite a shock," Rooster said, glancing at me.

"I could have done without it," I said.

Very entered the room and spotted me immediately.

"Oh, good, you're back," she said. "Cooter would like to have a talk with you. His room is the third door on the left."

"Sure," I said, getting to my feet.

236

"Try not to take too long," Rooster said. "We need to get going soon. We don't want Chef Claire making that trip back to the truck in the dark."

"I won't be long," I said, heading down the hall. I knocked softly on the door then slowly opened it. "You wanted to speak with me, Cooter?"

"Yeah, thanks for coming," he said, sitting up on the made bed. "How do you like my room?"

I glanced around at the bizarre collection of animal skins, children's toys, and dozens of comic books scattered on the bed and floor. It seemed more appropriate for an eight-year-old boy, but Cooter seemed proud of it, and I gave him a big smile.

"It's very nice," I said. "What do you want to talk about?"

"I'm scared, Suzy," he said, tearing up.

"It'll be okay, Cooter."

"Are you and Rooster gonna tell anybody?"

"What would we tell them?"

"Well, the truth for one," he said, grabbing and twisting the covers with both hands.

"The truth?" I said, rubbing my forehead.

Okay, Suzy. Decision time.

I took some time to organize my thoughts, swallowed hard, then started talking.

"As I remember it, Cooter, the truth is that you were showing Billows the cave, led him to where the path forms the Y, and then specifically asked him to take a look at the one on

237

the right. But I do believe that, at first, you were thinking about sending him down the path on the left. Then something inside you, probably something that comes from the way your mom and dad raised you to be a good person, you changed your mind and told him not to do that. The truth, as I see it, is that you *thought* about doing a bad thing, but you actually ended up *doing* the right thing."

"Do you really think so?" he said with a wide-eyed stare.

Man, the guy was apparently determined to make the conversation as tough as possible.

I scratched the back of my head and looked around the room. My eyes landed on the comic books, and I decided to try a different approach.

"You know how superheroes like Spiderman and Captain America sometimes do bad things?"

"Sure," Cooter said. "But only when they have to do something like save the planet."

"Exactly," I said, waiting for my neurons to get their act together. "And I'm sure those superheroes often think about doing even worse stuff and then change their mind."

"They do," Cooter said, nodding. "Iron Man just did that in the latest issue."

"Well, there you go," I said, smiling. "And like those superheroes, you saw Mr. Billows as a threat to your…"

"Planet?"

"Sure, sure. That's probably a good word for it," I said. "He was about to disrupt everything you know and love, and you got scared and turned protective. And while you wanted to do something to hurt him, eventually you decided you were better than that, and your own superhero qualities took over. Because that's what superheroes do."

"Yeah, they do, don't they?" Cooter said, beaming. "I think I'm starting to feel better."

"Good."

"Boy, I don't get scared too often," Cooter said, stretching his legs out in front of him.

"That's because you're a brave guy," I said. "Living way out here the way you do."

"That's the second time I've been scared this month," Cooter said. "I don't think that's ever happened before."

"What scared you the last time?"

"It was when that guy showed up, and he and Papa started shouting at each other," he said, frowning at the memory.

"Mr. Billows?" I said, my neurons twitching.

"No, it was some other guy. Papa and I were outside fixing the fence when this guy showed up. Papa made me walk away, but I could hear them screaming back and forth. Then the guy told Papa to watch out and then he left. It scared the heck out of me."

"Do you know what they were arguing about?"

"Not really," Cooter said. "But the guy kept yelling and swearing at Papa saying stay away from the cape, stay away from the cape. It didn't make any sense to me since he has wasn't wearing a cape, but it sure seemed important to him."

I flinched, and Cooter recoiled backward in the bed, startled.

"Are you okay, Suzy?"

"I'm fine," I said, my neurons on fire. "It's just a bit of a headache. Did your dad tell you what the fight was about?"

"Nah, Papa never talked about stuff like that. He told me not to worry about it and went back to work fixing the fence."

"What did the man look like?"

"He was really big. And his head was shaved. He looked funny because the cold air was making steam come off the top of his head. And he had this really big droopy mustache that had snow and ice all over it."

"You didn't hear his name, did you?"

"No, just a lot of yelling and swearing," Cooter said, reaching for a comic book.

He slowly opened the cover and was soon engrossed.

"Okay, Cooter," I said, heading toward the door. "I need to get going. It was nice seeing you. And try not to worry. I'm sure this will all quiet down soon."

"Thanks for talking to me," he said, glancing up from the comic book.

"No problem. I enjoyed it."

"And thanks for your help in the cave with the policeman."

"Don't mention it," I said, holding his eyes with mine. "To anybody."

# Chapter 25

We made our way back to Rooster's truck just before dark. Chef Claire, who ended up walking and carrying her skis after falling down three times in the first five minutes, climbed into the backseat and passed out, snoring softly.

"Can you live with it?" I said to Rooster who was staring out at the road.

"You mean, the alternate truth?" he said, glancing over.

"That's a good term for it," I said. "And there is a lot of truth in there."

"There is," he said, nodding. "And the kid did try to do the right thing. Eventually."

"Just not fast enough," I said. "I guess he'll have plenty of time to think about what he did and didn't do while he's living out there all by himself."

"Yeah, when you think about it, he is sort of in prison," Rooster said, choosing his words carefully. "You know, from an isolation standpoint."

"Except he's going to have several dogs to keep him company," I said. "I don't think you get that in prison."

"Hey, try not to nitpick," he said, laughing. "I'm trying to help us out here."

"Good point," I said, glancing into the backseat. "She's out."

"She is indeed," Rooster said. "I thought I might take you three out to dinner tomorrow night. It might be the last chance I get before you head to Cayman."

"That sounds good," I said. "C's?"

"Where else?" he said. "Chef Claire said she's doing an Italian special tomorrow. But she's taking the night off after she gets things organized in the kitchen."

"I'm in."

"I'm also thinking about taking the snowmobile out during the day. You feel like tagging along?"

"No, I've got something to do tomorrow. Road trip."

"Where are you going?"

"Cape Vincent."

"To see the Rossi woman?" Rooster said, glancing over.

"Yeah," I said, slowly nodding my head.

"Should I even ask?"

"Not yet," I said, glancing over at him. "But I'll tell you all about it tomorrow night." Then a lightbulb went off in my head. "Hey, why didn't we just take the snowmobiles out to the Friendly's place?"

"Because we needed the exercise," he said, staring out at the road.

"Speak for yourself."

Rooster pulled into the parking lot in front of the Inn, and I grimaced from a leg cramp as I climbed out.

"Do you think Jessie is going to sell the property to 3E?" I said, holding the door open.

"I do not," he said.

"But it's going to cost us more than we originally thought, isn't it?"

"Oh, yeah," Rooster said, nodding.

I closed the passenger door and opened the back door on my side. I gently shook Chef Claire by the shoulder.

"Hey, Sleeping Beauty. We're home."

Chef Claire slowly came to and yawned. Then she shook her head.

"I've got a headache," she said, climbing out of the truck.

"Me too," I said. "But probably for a different reason."

"I'm going up to the house to take a shower," she said, waving goodbye to Rooster.

"You sure you don't want a little nip before you go?" Rooster said as he held up a glass jar of the clear liquid.

"Funny," Chef Claire said, staggering slightly as she made her way to the path that led up to the house.

"No sipping from that jar until you get home. See you tomorrow," I said, closing the back door and waving.

I watched Rooster drive off then headed inside the Inn through the front door. Jill was sitting behind the reception desk and working on the computer.

"Hey, how was your day?" she said.

"Eventful," I said. "Where's Josie?"

"Where do you think?" Jill said, laughing.

I nodded and headed for the condo area where I found Josie sitting on the floor next to the Otterhound. She was stroking Gabby's head and giving the sleeping puppies a loving stare.

"Hey," I said, standing in the doorway. "What did I miss?"

"Not much," Josie said. "I had a couple annual exams this afternoon, and I had to stitch up the Smith's spaniel that somehow managed to run into a barbed wire fence."

"Ow," I said, frowning. "How's the dog doing?"

"She's fine," Josie said. "Andy took her home a couple hours ago. I've spent most of the day out here watching these guys."

"How are they doing?"

"Couldn't be better," she said. "But delivering this litter took a lot out of her. That's three, and I think that's probably enough. Do you think we can get the widow Friendly to agree to have her spayed?"

"We'll need to get Cooter's permission for that," I said. "But I don't think that will be a problem."

"He's taking the dog?"

"Yes, and two of the puppies," I said. "Mother and daughter are moving to Florida and don't want to take the dogs with them."

"Interesting," she said. "I take it she wasn't thrilled with the fact that the puppies aren't purebred?"

"She was not," I said. "But she got over it in a hurry. Suddenly, money is the least of her concerns."

"So, how was your day?"

"Well, let's see, I spent way too much of it on skis, had an interesting chat with Cooter about the inner conflicts lurking within every superhero, and Chef Claire got hammered on moonshine."

"She got drunk?" Josie said, laughing.

"She's up at the house taking a shower trying to sober up," I said, then frowned. "Oh, and Herman Billows fell down a hole in a cave."

"And?" she said, raising an eyebrow.

"And the Chief is out there with a rescue crew trying to recover the body."

"Recover it? How far did he fall?"

"Five Mississippi," I said.

"That's a lot of Mississippi," she said, frowning.

"That's what we thought. Rooster wanted to tag along with the rescue crew so he could see what's at the bottom."

"You mean, besides Billows' body, right?"

"Nothing gets past you."

"They wouldn't let Rooster go with them?"

"No," I said, laughing. "That's all they'd need. Oh, by the way, he's taking us to dinner tomorrow night."

"Works for me. Chef Claire's doing Italian."

"And Rooster's looking for somebody to go snowmobiling with tomorrow if you're interested."

"No, he drives way too fast for me," she said, shaking her head. "Are you going?"

"No, I have to go to Cape Vincent."

"To see the Rossi woman?"

"Yeah."

"Okay," Josie said, staring at me. "Please tell me she wasn't the one who killed Friendly."

"No, she wasn't."

"But you've figured out who did?"

"Yeah, I'm pretty sure I have. Not that I can ever prove it."

"You have been busy."

"Yeah, it's been a day."

*Chapter 26*

Sofia Rossi greeted the Chief and me at the door with a confused look on her face. Her Rottweiler barked and growled his severe displeasure at our unannounced pop in.

"Hi, Sofia. Hey, Stinky," I said, kneeling down in the doorway and slowly extending my bandaged hand toward the dog.

"That's not very nice," the Chief whispered, keeping a close eye on the Rottweiler with the throaty grumble.

"It's his name," I said, scratching one of the dog's ears.

"That's right," he said. "How could I forget that?"

"Please, come in," Sofia said, staring at Chief Abrams' badge.

She stepped back from the door, and we entered the warm house. The Rottweiler followed at our heels as we entered the living room, removed our coats then sat down.

"Can I get you anything?"

"No, I'm good," I said, smiling at her.

"Nothing for me, thanks," Chief Abrams said, cautiously stroking the dog's head.

"What brings you out here on such a cold and windy day?" Sofia said.

"We'd like to talk to you," I said.

"Is this some sort of official visit?" she said to the Chief.

"No, it's not," Chief Abrams said. "Actually, I'm just here to keep an eye on Suzy."

"Funny," I said, making a face at him. "We'd like to talk to you about what happened to Skitch Friendly."

She immediately began to tear up, and I waited until she wiped her eyes and regained her composure.

"What about Skitch?" she said.

"You two were very close, weren't you?" I said.

Sofia stared at me, then shrugged and nodded her head.

"We were certainly getting there. How did you know that?"

"At first, it was just a guess," I said. "But after the Otterhound had her litter, I sort of put it together."

"The Otterhound had a litter of puppies?" she said, frowning. "I find that hard to believe. We weren't planning a litter until the spring."

"Yeah, I know," I said, stroking the Rottweiler's head. "But this guy had other ideas."

"What?" she said, stunned. "You think Stinky is the father of her litter?"

"Yeah, it certainly appears that way," I said. "And I didn't understand how it was possible, given how closely the two of you were working together on purebred Otterhounds. Leaving the dogs unsupervised was an odd thing to do, but I imagine you and Skitch were busy doing something else."

Sofia ran a hand through her hair then chuckled.

"Neither one of us had a clue Gabby was in heat," she said. "What do the puppies look like?"

"They're gorgeous," I said. "But they're still very young. They haven't even opened their eyes yet."

"How many in the litter?"

"Six."

"What's going to happen with them?" Sofia said.

"Gabby and two of the puppies are going with Skitch's son, Cooter," I said. "We'll put the other four up for adoption when they're ready."

"I'd like one of them," Sofia said.

I wasn't sure if she wanted a puppy as a playmate for the Rottweiler or as a remembrance of Skitch Friendly. It was probably a lot of both.

"Sure, I'll have somebody give you a call in about six weeks," I said.

"Okay," she said. "I can't imagine you came here just to confirm that I was involved with Skitch."

"No, we didn't," I said. "But how serious was the relationship?"

"It was pretty intense," she said. "But destined to remain…episodic. He was considering divorce, but there was no way he was ever going to leave what he called his *palace in the woods*. I've never seen it, but I certainly wasn't going to move out there. Have you been out to his place?"

"We have," the Chief said.

"What's it like?"

"Remote," the Chief said. "But apart from the lack of electricity and running water, it's actually very nice."

"Definitely not something I could handle," Sofia said, then studied my expression. "You're holding something back. What is it?"

"We don't think Skitch's death was an accident," I said.

"You think he was murdered?" Sofia said, glancing back and forth at us, surprised.

"We do," the Chief said.

"You can't possibly believe that I had anything to do with it," Sofia said.

"No, not a chance," I said, shaking my head. "Is your ex-husband a large man, Sofia?"

Sofia sat back in her chair, stunned.

"My ex-husband?"

"Yes. Is he a big guy?"

"As a matter of fact, he is."

"Bald with a big, drooping mustache?"

"Yes," she whispered. "How on earth did you know that?"

"Because Skitch's son watched an argument between his dad and your ex-husband a couple of weeks ago," I said. "Is your ex-husband violent?"

"He certainly can be," she said after a long pause. "Peter's capable of anything. He'd been stalking me. And we had a couple of confrontations where he threatened me. He'd found out

I was seeing someone, but I had no idea he knew who it was. Do you really think he might have killed Skitch?"

"I think it's very possible," I said.

"Did you call the police and let them know your ex-husband was stalking you?" Chief Abrams said.

"No, I just called my father," she said, shrugging. "As a cop, you might be familiar with his work."

"Mikey the Mechanic," the Chief said, nodding.

"An unfortunate nickname, but that's him," she said. "I called my dad, and he said he would take care of it."

"And?" the Chief said.

"And I haven't seen Peter in several days," Sofia said. "My father probably convinced him to take a nice long vacation. Perhaps somewhere near the ocean."

"Or under it," I whispered.

"Yes," Sofia said, flashing a small smile that made the hairs on the back of my neck stand up. "Or under it. Do you have any proof that Peter killed Skitch?"

"Absolutely none," the Chief said. "And I doubt we ever will."

"It doesn't matter," Sofia said. "I'm sure justice has prevailed."

It was a funny way to say that her father recently had her ex-husband whacked, but I wasn't going to quibble. Especially after the look she'd just given me. I brushed my hand across the back of my neck to get the hairs down. Then my neurons flared.

"Is Walter back from his trip yet? I believe he said he was going to Scranton," I said.

"I'm afraid Walter no longer works for me," Sofia said.

"You called your father?" I said, cocking my head at her.

Sofia laughed and shook her head.

"No, it was nothing like that. Walter called the other day and said he had decided to move back to Florida."

"Just like that, huh?" I said, ignoring the look the Chief was giving me.

"Just like that," she said. "You don't know anyone who's comfortable working with dogs, do you?"

"Nobody that comfortable," I said, shaking my head.

"What?"

"Nothing," I said, glancing at the Chief who nodded at the door. "We should get going. Thanks for your time, Sofia."

"Thank you for giving me some closure," she said. "And for the puppy."

"No problem," I said, standing up and extending my hand. "We'll call you as soon as they're ready."

"It was nice meeting you, Chief Abrams," Sofia said, shaking his hand.

"You too," he said, putting his coat on. Then he leaned down to pet the Rottweiler. "He's a good dog. But why did you give him that name?"

"It was my father's decision," Sofia said, laughing. "He thought it was perfect for him."

"And you don't argue with your father, right?"

"I wouldn't recommend it."

# Epilogue

"Hold still. You're such a big baby."

"You're hurting me. You could crack walnuts with those hands."

"Suzy, I just came out of surgery with Gabby where I put a plate in her leg along with six screws to hold it in place, and she complained less than you."

"How's she doing?"

"She doing fine," Josie said, removing another stitch from my hand. "I would have preferred to hold off until she stopped nursing, but I didn't want to wait any longer to get that leg fixed."

"Will the anesthesia impact her milk?" I said, then winced. "Ow."

"Oh, sorry about that one. I got a bit of skin," Josie said, chuckling. "No, it shouldn't be a problem. But just to be safe, I asked Sammy and Jill to bottle feed the puppies for a few days. And Gabby can use the rest. The poor girl has been through a lot."

"She certainly has," I said, glancing down at the half-moon of puffy, red skin that ran between my thumb and index finger. "That's going to be an ugly scar."

"It's going to be a beautiful scar," Josie said, removing the final stitch. She tossed the tweezers on a metal tray then used a wet wipe on my hand. "There you go. Good as new."

I examined my hand then shrugged.

"Thanks. But I still say your bedside manner needs work."

"Yeah, I really need to start working on that," she said, punching me on the shoulder.

"Funny," I said, glancing out the window. "It's snowing again."

"I didn't know it had stopped," she said, shrugging. "But tomorrow night we'll be sitting around the pool relaxing."

"Actually, we'll be sitting around my mom's pool," I said. "She called this morning and said she's throwing an arrival party for us."

"That sounds like fun," Josie said, removing her lab coat. "When is Max getting in?"

"He got in today," I said. "He's going to stay with my mom and Paulie tonight."

"Uh-oh," Josie said, laughing.

"Yeah, I know. She'll have an unchecked opportunity to sprinkle grandkid references into every conversation."

"Did you talk with Sammy and Jill about Gabby and the puppies?"

"I did. As we agreed, Gabby stays right here until the puppies are eight weeks. They'll give Cooter the instructions you wrote down about how to handle Gabby until he's sure her leg is completely healed. And he gets the pick of the litter. Then Sofia picks the one she wants. And the other three go up for adoption. That is if you're sure you don't want to keep one."

"No, for the last time, we're not keeping one," Josie said, shaking her head. "Unless they don't get adopted. But that's highly unlikely. They're going to be great looking dogs."

"Yeah, I think they are," I said, rubbing the scar on my hand. "You ready for dinner?"

Josie rolled her eyes at me as she hung her lab coat on a hook and headed for the back door of the Inn. We headed up to the house and found Chef Claire in the living room sitting in front of the fire with Rooster and Chief Abrams. Chef Claire got up and poured wine for us.

"Thanks," I said, taking a sip. "Have you finished packing?"

"I finished a week ago," Chef Claire said.

"I wish I was going with you," Rooster said. "This has the look of a *very* long winter. But I guess I'll be down there soon enough."

"Why wait?" I said.

"Sure, just fly out with us tomorrow," Chef Claire said.

"That's a great idea," Josie said. "Your shepherd is going to be staying with Millie, right?"

"Actually, she's going to be housesitting for me," Rooster said, frowning. "I don't know. It's pretty short notice."

"Got your passport?" I said.

"I do."

"Then give Millie a call, pack a bag when you get home tonight, and by this time tomorrow you'll be sunburned and buzzed on Mudslides," Josie said, then glanced at Chef Claire. "Or you can bring the jar of shine along. I know Chef Claire would love that."

"Shut it."

"Why not?" Rooster said, shrugging. "Okay, I'm in."

"And I'll be stuck here shoveling snow, freezing and bored out of my mind," the Chief said.

"Hang in there, Chief," Josie said. "Maybe you'll get lucky, and they'll be a crime wave."

"Yeah, thanks," the Chief said. "We're planning to come down the first two weeks in February if that works with your schedule."

"Our schedule," Josie said, glancing over at me. "That's so sweet. He thinks we have a schedule down there."

"We barely have a calendar," Chef Claire said, laughing.

"Oh, I almost forgot," Rooster said, reaching into his coat pocket and handing me a thick envelope. "Jessie signed off today on the sale."

"That was quick," I said, removing a folded document from the envelope.

"They're anxious to get on the road," Rooster said. "And she liked my last offer."

"When do you need the money?" I said.

"I already paid her," Rooster said. "You can give me your share whenever you get a chance."

"Why wait?" I said, rummaging through my bag for my checkbook. "How much do I owe you?"

"The sales price is on the first page," he said. "You'll need to divide it by three."

"Yeah, thanks for the tip," I said, making a face at him. I glanced down at the number then frowned.

"Really?"

"Yeah, I know," he said.

I shrugged, wrote the check, and handed it to him. Josie stared at me then looked at Chef Claire.

"Did you see that?"

"I did," Chef Claire said. "I give more thought to writing the check for my phone bill."

"There was nothing to think about," I said, tossing the checkbook back into my bag. "It's no big deal."

"It was so sweet of you to buy that cabin for Cooter," Josie said with a big grin. "I see a new hat in your future."

"Yeah, and maybe a pair of matching slippers," Chef Claire deadpanned.

"You can both stop now," I said.

"Well, you guys did a good thing," the Chief said. "On behalf of environmentalists everywhere, I thank you."

"I still want to get a look at the bottom of that cave," Rooster said.

"The guys on the rescue crew said it's pretty amazing down there," the Chief said. "Apparently, there's a whole other set of caves down there next to the underground spring."

"Did they say how deep the hole is?" Rooster said.

"It's just under four hundred feet," the Chief said.

"Wow. I'd love to see it," Rooster said.

"Me too," Chef Claire said.

Josie and I stared at her in disbelief.

"What?" Chef Claire said. "I would."

"Knock yourself out," Josie said, shaking her head.

"We should all do it," Chef Claire said. "Sometime next summer."

"That's a great idea," Rooster said.

"Yeah," I said, laughing. "I'll let you know."

We heard a knock on the kitchen door, then Freddie called out.

"We're in here," I said.

Freddie came into the living room, his coat and boots already off.

"Man, it's brutal coming back to this weather. Miami was perfect the whole time I was there."

"There's wine," Chef Claire said. "Help yourself."

"I think I will do just that. Thanks."

He poured a glass, took a sip, and slowly rocked on his heels as he glanced back and forth at us.

"So, what did I miss while I was gone?"

I looked around the room, noticed the small smiles on display, then glanced up at Freddie and shrugged.

"Oh, you know, just the usual."

*My good friend and bestselling author, Dianne Harman, has a new book out and I'd like to share a bit about it here. Murder in San Francisco is book number eight in her popular Liz Lucas Cozy Mystery Series, and if you aren't already one of Dianne's fans, I think you'll soon understand why she is a USA Today Bestselling Author and seven-time Amazon All-Star.*

*And she thought she'd have a bit of fun and use me as the murder victim in the book. But I guess it could have been worse. In the book, I'm incredibly rich and live a long time before I get taken out.*

*Enjoy!*

# Murder in San Francisco

Murder in San Francisco- Get it here!

**When a child is conceived and born after his father's murder, is that child a legal heir to his millions?**

Michelle D'Amato's pregnant with San Francisco millionaire octogenarian Bernie Snow's baby, but he's dead, and a lot of people would like to see her dead as well, so her baby can't lay claim to his vast estate. Was that why he was murdered? And if so, who killed him? Was it for his money or revenge?

Bernie had threatened to disinherit his ne'er-do-well son, Larry, and his estranged daughter, Toni, so maybe they murdered him before he could carry out his threat. Then there's Toni's husband, Rocco, who has ties to the mob and is desperate for money. What about Jim, who's still angry with Bernie after he was forced out of the electronics company he and Bernie founded? Or even Dr. T, who operates a sperm bank and facilitated Michelle's pregnancy. He knew her future born child would have a legitimate claim to Bernie's estate, even if she didn't, and that was a lot of money.

Join Liz, Roger, and their dog, Winston, in a race against time as they search for the killer before Michelle either suffers a miscarriage caused by stress or is the next murder victim.